They don't come nicer than Jerry Cayce. Just ask his family.

Yet something is about to go wrong . . . horribly wrong.

Someone's been leaving presents for the police department . . . with gruesome contents. . . .

People are disappearing, but no bodies can be found. . . .

But Jerry knows a little secret. A secret he keeps locked up in his word processor and in the darkest depths of his mind.

Now, though, it's a secret that's coming out in one hacked-off bloody clue after another. . . .

BLACKOUT

Seth Kindler

▼

BLACKOUT

A SIGNET BOOK

SIGNET
Published by the Penguin Group
Penguin Books USA Inc., 375 Hudson Street,
New York, New York 10014, U.S.A.
Penguin Books Ltd, 27 Wrights Lane,
London W8 5TZ, England
Penguin Books Australia Ltd, Ringwood,
Victoria, Australia
Penguin Books Canada Ltd, 10 Alcorn Avenue,
Toronto, Ontario, Canada M4V 3B2
Penguin Books (N.Z.) Ltd, 182–190 Wairau Road,
Auckland 10, New Zealand

Penguin Books Ltd, Registered Offices:
Harmondsworth, Middlesex, England
First published by Signet,
an imprint of Dutton Signet,
a division of Penguin Books USA Inc.

First Printing, October, 1994
10 9 8 7 6 5 4 3 2 1

 REGISTERED TRADEMARK—MARCA REGISTRADA

Printed in the United States of America

PUBLISHER'S NOTE
This is a work of fiction. Names, characters, places, and incidents either are the product of the author's imagination or are used fictitiously, and any resemblance to actual persons, living or dead, events, or locales is entirely coincidental.

BOOKS ARE AVAILABLE AT QUANTITY DISCOUNTS WHEN USED TO PROMOTE PRODUCTS OR SERVICES. FOR INFORMATION PLEASE WRITE TO PREMIUM MARKETING DIVISION, PENGUIN BOOKS USA INC., 375 HUDSON STREET, NEW YORK, NEW YORK 10014.

AUTHOR'S NOTE

I'd like to thank my brother, the English Literature professor, for his insight and the suggestions that made the plot work.

Also, anyone who is acquainted with the Police Department division of Nashville's Criminal Justice Center will quickly recognize that I've taken liberties with the homicide personnel, the locations of their offices, and the views from their windows.

Oh, if I had Orpheus' voice and poetry
with which to move the Dark Maid and her Lord,
I'd call you back, dear love, from the world below.
I'd go down there for you. Charon or the grim
King's dog could not prevent me then
from carrying you up into the fields of light.

(Euripides, from *Alcestis*, 438 B.C.)

CHAPTER ONE

I

"What the hell is it?"

A slab of meat the size of two large fists lay on the morgue's porcelain autopsy table. A crevice bisected it into smoothly rounded halves that were connected at one end by a thin bridge of tissue. The slab looked slightly familiar, but Farley couldn't quite coax its identity to the front of his mind.

"It's an anus."

The gaunt pathologist adjusted the halogen work light and carefully unfolded the collar of the green frock he had just donned. The words fell hard.

"You gotta be kidding!" But the clarity that had been eluding the detective popped into focus. "Oh, sweet God Almighty, Sanger! It is." He stepped backward, puffing and swishing his arms in disgust.

The pathologist's spidery fingers dramatically plucked a stainless steel probe from a row of instruments arranged on a green cloth. The little finger stuck out like an English socialite drinking tea as he carefully spread the two rounded lobes. The crevice was gently shaped to reconnect the open ends that had formerly hugged the coccyx. White table showed through the rounded opening.

"It's a beauty, wouldn't you agree?" He glanced up at the cop and waited for a reaction. There was none. Shining his voice with sterility he continued, using the probe to point and prod. "What we have here is the distal four inches of the alimentary canal. It is comprised of two and one-half inches of the intestinum rectum and an inch and a half of the anal canal. As you can see, it includes sections of the glutei maximi and the levator ani. Notice the . . ."

"I . . . see . . . an asshole, Sanger"—Farley had found his voice again—"and it's pathetically disgusting!"

Sanger's black eyes had carefully discarded all emotion. One of them peered at the detective over the top of crooked dissection glasses. The long head looked like the air had been sucked out of it, and the skin had become tightly stretched over the bones. He knew he looked like a B-horror-movie actor, and in the morgue setting he enjoyed playing the part.

The deliberate funeral-parlor, soft tenor voice wouldn't leave it alone. Unmollified, he turned his attention back to the meat and continued, "Asshole—rectum—anus—bum—touchhole—shit plunker. If it were from a Paramecium caudatum, we'd call it a cytopyge; a chicken, we'd call it part of the cloaca. If it were a . . ."

"Sanger!"

The doctor looked up once more from the specimen and this time gave Farley a short, left-sided grin. The crooked glasses hung on his nose by a thread. No one had ever seen Sanger's glasses fall off, and every once in a while the lunatic thought would bounce through Farley's mind that the man purposely glued them there just to make the diabolical doctor character a little more eccentric.

Sanger straightened and said, "We'll do blood work and a full scatalogical workup on the skin residue. It might tell us something, but I doubt it."

"Gawd. How could anyone cut something like that?"

Farley had seen a great deal of gore in eighteen years of police work—meaty highway accidents, bludgeon and chop-chop homicides, splattered jumpers, blown brains—but the realization of what was on the table brought a roller coaster's first plunge wave of acid from bowels to throat. He hammered it back into his stomach with sheer willpower.

The pathologist removed the probe and tossed it into an empty steel pan. The clank echoed sharply off the room's green tiles. Straightening, he brushed a long, greasy lock of black hair from his face with his sleeve. Farley couldn't ever remember seeing the man when he didn't need a haircut—or look like he'd just swallowed a dozen razor blades and a bottle of iodine.

Sanger pulled off the surgical gloves. "D'know, Joe." The soft voice was gone. "Have to have a strong stomach and a very sharp knife. It's a man—too much hair to be a woman. If it were a woman, we could safely call it a disaster. Get it? Dis-assed-her?"

"Cute, Sanger. Why would anybody want to . . ."

The doctor's gaze went back to the meat in response to a freshly turned memory. He interrupted, "Look at this cut here." He retrieved the probe from the pan and pointed to one of the hacked edges.

Farley leaned in once more. The faint smell . . .

"See these even striae? Had to be the backside of the knife sawing."

"So?"

"Probably a hunting-survival knife with serrations opposite the cutting edge."

"Rambo."

"A Rambo reamer."

"Rambo reamer."

Farley left the morgue, his stomach slopping like a kettle of hot grease. Walking down the long hall to the parking lot, he loosened his tie and took off his coat. Even a quarter of the new bottle of Maalox stashed in the glove compartment didn't help.

The small box had been labeled "POLICE" in Magic Marker. The night shift had found it on the lobby's information desk. There hadn't been a clue as to how it'd got there. It had just appeared.

The slab of meat had been wrapped in wax paper. Forensics had gone over everything with the laser. Had there been enough trace elements left on the paper, the laser would have excited them into a glow

and Jeeters had already drunk six cups. The other men in the office had to guard against the pot running empty. If Jeeters made a new pot, he would put in three packages of coffee, making the stuff strong enough to hype a horse. He normally drank between twenty and thirty cups a day, and that was just while he was at work.

"No. You find out what it was?"

"Asshole."

"Well, thank you, good Christian brother. If I'm an asshole, I hope you can keep your dick in your pants."

Farley looked at him and grinned.

"It was a human solid-waste orifice."

Jeeter's hatchet face registered the shock as an oversized Adam's apple bobbed three or four times. Beetling, thick eyebrows bumped up and down in their own rhythm beneath thick worry waves on his forehead. "Jesus, Joe! No kidding? Those little clumps of meat?"

"Male."

"I thought it looked familiar."

"Why didn't you tell us what it was then?" Farley asked, dropping several While You Were Out messages in the wastebasket while fingering his Rolodex. No answer was expected.

"Gadly! Cut it right out?" Jeeters was standing at the coffee machine pouring. Mostly to himself, he said slowly, ". . . Worse than watching your mother get gang-banged by the First Baptist Men's Choir." He unconsciously scrunched his face and rear end, visualizing the operation. It cost him a burned finger as the coffee slipped over the side of the too-full cup.

"Yut." Farley was still inattentive. "Hey, who was that shrink at Vandy we talked to a couple years ago—the one who worked up the profile of The Thrasher? You remember?"

Two years before, Nashville had had a wave of murders that had made national news headlines. The three-hundred-fifty-pound killer had got high on life by stomping and kicking semiconscious derelicts to death with heavy steel-toed boots. Most of the poor souls had given up the ghost when The Thrasher administered his coup de grace—a jump to their chests from a height of five or six feet that shattered breastbone into heart.

"Hallspring. Saul Hallspring—something like that."

"You got a number?"

"It's in my Rolodex. Look under H. The guy wrote a book about it. You ever read it, Joe?"

"No. That kind of stuff scares me. Here it is. Samuel Holbrook."

II

Ron Creed slammed the bolt shut on the rifle's receiver and shot the two telephone books leaning against the cellar wall. The slight cough from the gun made the books jump. A few yellow paper shreds fluttered to the dusty cement floor.

"Not bad. Not bad at all. Better than mine. Couldn't hear that over twenty feet away."

He walked over and picked up the *The Real Yellow Pages* for greater Nashville, which was stacked in front of the white pages. Both books were about two inches thick. The bullet was buried in the *H*'s of the second book. The lead bullet was mutilated but intact.

He repeated the experiment using the dum-dum he'd made by sawing a shallow groove across the tip of the lead with a serrated butcher knife. This time, the bullet didn't penetrate but a few pages into the second book, and it had disintegrated a great deal.

"Nice for close, but not accurate for more than a few dozen feet. I'll stick with the hollow points— maybe filled with a little mercury. Slow death, but unavoidable. They'll think the CIA or the Russians did it."

Creed had not shot a .22 extensively since he was a kid. Most of his shooting now was with high-powered rifles and a ten- or twelve-power scope. He enjoyed the kick and the implied power that came with the reach. With his 220 Swift, he could hole a quarter from two hundred yards or a grapefruit from five hundred yards if there was no wind.

But a silencer didn't work on the Swift or anything else that was faster than the speed of sound. There were suppressors for the larger bore guns, and they would provide silence at the gun's barrel, but when the bullet hit the target, it instantly went subsonic, and the laws of physics mandated a loud bang. A totally silent weapon had to have a subsonic load. The spooks and militaries had higher caliber loads purposely undercharged for a silencer, but unless you loaded your own or worked for Uncle Sam, the .22 long was the best thing readily available that was slow enough not to break the sound barrier.

He'd driven all the way to Memphis to a gun show to steal the silencer after experimenting with several homemade models and finding them cumbersome—plastic soft-drink bottles filled with insulation, PVC pipe lined with glued-in washers, potatoes. John Q. Citizen couldn't buy a silencer without filling out the forms for a Class II license and going through the Feds, and then it was absolutely illegal to use the thing. To hell with them. Stealing it had been a lot easier than it should have been. All it had taken was a diversion—lighting a cigarette, casually throwing the cupped cherry bomb under a dealer's table with no one looking. The dealer selling the suppressors had jumped out of his skin along with everybody else in the hall—certain that some idiot had fired a live round. With every head in the place turned, Creed had grabbed the two silencers that were on the table and slowly walked away through an agitated crowd. Tonight the kill would be completely silent—better than last time.

III

Farley walked up the front steps of the Vanderbilt Medical School's psychiatric wing and opened the door for a couple of nurses who had followed him across the quad. He had been shamelessly eavesdropping on their conversation, staying just far enough ahead to keep them from passing. They were speculating on the weekend. A stockbroker had invited them to go sailing on Percy Priest Lake—just the three of them. The question was, if the stockbroker wanted to, would they go threezies with him.

The turned down the opposite hall just as they were about to make a decision, and Farley almost followed them to hear the outcome.

About half the length of the building away, he could see the office door on the right. Next to it there was a large bulletin board overgrown with notices and posters. The door was open, and an undergrad secretary, plugged into a dictation machine, was finger flailing an IBM Selectric almost as fast as she was chewing gum.

"Yes?" she asked without looking up.

"Inspector Farley. Appointment, Dr. Holbrook."

"He's free. Go on in." She never missed a beat with the gum or the typewriter.

Holbrook's back was to him, and Farley knocked on the open door's casing.

"Yo."

The psychiatrist turned around in a laboring desk chair to reveal a face that resembled a wrinkly dog. Like the rest of him, it was very overweight, corrugating fiercely from the forehead down the full length and breadth to puddle in an accordion chin. Flat nose. Exophthalmic eyes. Closest resemblances were to a Boston terrier that favored Peter Lorre.

"Inspector Farley. Come in. Have a chair." There was a sideways, well-padded chair butted up against the front of the desk. Evidently, Holbrook put a great deal of emphasis on comfort while seated. His own chair was extravagantly padded. He extended a hand.

"Doctor."

Farley took the hand and then handed him the enlarged eight-by-ten glossy that he took from a manila envelope.

"Doc, what do you think about a psycho who would cut out a man's anus?"

Holbrook calmly took the picture and turned it ninety degrees—once—twice—then back—as if it would magically focus for him from a different perspective. The lobes of meat were posed spread open, the white porcelain table showing through the one-inch, or so, hole.

"Oh, yes. Mmmmmm. Ouch."

"Yup."

"How did you come by it?"

"It was left at our front desk. No one saw who delivered it. I'm Homicide. I don't imagine the guy it belongs to is alive anymore."

"How was it wrapped?"

"Wax paper. Cardboard box."

"Helluvan anal fixation."

"Freud."

"Yup. Letter? Note?"

"Nope."

"Any leads?"

"Nope. Thought you might have some ideas."

"Finger. Scalp. A trophy. Hmmm," Holbrook mused, still turning the picture, but not really looking at it. "The practice dates back to the beginning of man. They've found evidence in Africa, China, Turkey—lots of places. In the Irish peat bogs they once dug up a preserved body that had a row of mummified ears on a leather throng around the neck. In the Hellenic Wars, the warriors used to cut off the enemies' penes, dry them, and string them on a chain around their waist. Scared the hell out of the enemy."

"It would scare the hell out of me."

"Most civilizations at war today still mutilate the dead. Cut off ears, gouge out eyes. Cut off the penis and stuff it in the mouth. Arabs, Africans, Central America."

"Gotta smart."

"I've never heard of this before, though." He stopped rotating the picture, looked briefly once more at it, and handed it back to the detective. "Probably insecure—transferring—cutting out a hole—removing a pitfall that can swallow you. Maybe guilt—eliminate temptation—one less place to stick a phallus."

"Maybe."

"Real anal fixation. Maybe latent homosexual. Despises the world—all assholes to him. Probably did time in some place where there was authority over him: prison, military, some kind of institution where there were supervisors—maybe bureaucrats. You don't have the rest of the body?"

"Not yet."

"That might tell us a lot more. How he killed his victim—cleanly—one shot to the back of the head, or to the heart, with a gun; or messy—knife, ax, hit-and-run; what kind of victim—big, little. You know these things as well as I."

"Yeah. It's not much to go on. I thought you might have run into something like it before. Let you know when we have more. Thanks." Farley stood and extended his hand.

"Do that, please. This may be a new one for the case studies."

CHAPTER TWO

The only light in the attic room came from the ghoul-green screen of the word processor. Outside, unnoticed, a perfunctory dawn had come and gone. Other than slippers that resembled stuffed bears wearing hats, the author was clad only in foxed Jockeys. Words marched across the screen to the beat of complicated plastic cadences. He continued . . .

I

Creed buttoned the top button of his camo jacket and pulled the dripping hat a little farther down over his head. It had been raining on and off for a week, and although the temperature had remained in the high sixties and low seventies . . .

* * *

"Daddy, are we going to the lake?"

"In a little while, sweetheart. Daddy needs to work just a wee bit longer. You go tell Mommy I'll be ready in about an hour."

"Daddy, please hurry."

"I will, sweetie. It'll be a short hour."

. . . the accumulated dampness gnawed at the core of a man's bones. There were at least a dozen large puddles spread around the gravel parking lot, some straddled by the half-dozen cars. The orange mercury-vapor lamp highlighted an ephemeral clump of mist as it trailed slowly across the lot.

He had parked the truck on an overgrown road used at one time to log the thick woods that surrounded the studio. The road was only fifty yards from where he crouched. The mists cleared temporarily to reveal an uprooted sign leaning against the back wall of the building. Scrofulous lettering announced "PINEWOOD RECORDING STUDIOS," but the only pine trees in the area were the rust-tipped plantings on either side of the sign's former location on the front lawn. It was well after midnight. Creed shivered, hoping that inside . . .

II

... The vocal group was on the last chorus of the last song. Inside the control room, the producer and engineer were hunched in plush executive chairs, elbows resting on the padded leather edge of the six-by-four-foot console that was studded with hundreds of knobs and buttons. The only light in the room came from the meters and indicators on the "board" and its stacks of subordinating equipment. It gave the room the appearance of being lit by an almost-dead fire.

"Can you jeeggle the pye-ana up just a haar?"

The voice came from huge speakers embedded in the front wall.

The engineer punched the talk-back button at the right end of the console and said, "Up the pye-ana? Sointenly!" A microphone on the console sent the message to four pairs of earphones.

Through the large picture window, four singers were framed in the dim studio light. They were huddling around a microphone and a lighted music stand that held a set of double-spaced lyrics. The margins and most of the spaces between the lines contained numbers and words that had been scribbled through, rewritten, and rescribbled through a number of times. There was hardly a blank space on the sheet that wasn't covered with penciling, including the snide, hastily scribbled one-liners about the producer, the song, and the artist who had a lisp and couldn't sing in tune.

The engineer reached lazily for the cue knob that turned up the piano on the earphone cue. It was, at least, the tenth time he had been asked to change the mix. One singer would want more drums, then another would want more piano; then a third would want the whole thing turned down and the live voices turned up.

"Okay, Mousies, last-chorus stack. It's Miller Time, so sang purr-dy." The accent feigning, including "pye-ana" and "haar," was an indicator of fatigue—and boredom.

"Wait! Wait! Can we get the unison line in the verse? It wasn't too together, but it was pretty out of tune—at least in the alto section." The alto was wrinkling her nose, deriding her own performance.

"Sounded good in here, but, hey, we aim to please. Punching the third line of the verse." He hit a sequence of numbers on the remote console, then "REWIND," and the twenty-four-track machine backed up a few dozen feet; then he hit "PLAY," and the music started exactly four bars before the third line in the verse. The track had been recorded the previous afternoon by a six-piece rhythm section, and it included the scratch vocals sung by a truck driver from Ohio who had saved and borrowed to scrape together thirty thousand dollars to make his own country record. The man, already well into his forties, had taken out a second mortgage on his home in abject belief that he could make it if only given this one last chance. Unfortunately, he might as well have poured the money into the Ohio River. One in a hundred singers had the talent and the looks; one in a thousand was in the right place at the right time—when one of the labels was looking to invest some "development" money in a "product"; one in ten thousand hopefuls had the charisma to be awarded the major-label backing and the sustained millions of dollars spent on publicity, not including ten to thirty grand a week in promotion to the radio stations and cable TV companies. Stardom was a product—the more money invested in promoting the product, the more money was made; and to make it big usually took millions.

A split second before the third line in the verse, the engineer's finger flicked at another square button on the remote and the button turned a dull red. The group began singing with their first track on a unison "Ooh" that was a countermelody to what the artist was singing. Now eight voices instead of four, the sound was significantly thickened. The truck driver sang the last line of the verse by himself, and the band went into the walkup to the chorus. There was a line of "Ahs" behind the artist on the first two lines of the chorus, he sang the third line by himself, then the group sang the last line with him . . .

* * *

"This is the last time that I'll be leavin' you."

For the overweight bass singer with the long hair and short captain's beard, it would be the last time.

III

It was almost one A.M. The session must be about finished. Creed's stomach began to curdle, and he felt the diarrhetic need to defecate. It would pass. It always did.

He took the scope cover off the Nighthawk infrared scope just as the back door opened to dump a splash of new light on the mud and puddles. Two women emerged and tiptoed across the parking lot in the mud.

"Is it ever gonna stop rainin'?"

"I hope so—by this weekend. We're supposed to play Starwood with Dolly. It'll cut down on the crowd if they have to bring umbrellas." The woman's southern accent emphasized the *um* instead of the *brell*.

The ladies got into one car, and as it puddle-smashed around the corner of the building, the studio door opened once more. The producer and the tenor stood backlit and laughing. The condition of the parking lot quickly changed their focus, and the laughing died in just a few, short spurts. The trip through the mud was made with percussive "Shit!"s.

Creed knew that Robbie Gilson, the bass singer, would most certainly remain behind to check his answering machine's evening messages. Robbie had an undying obsession to know if anyone had called him, and the singer would unabashedly hog the phone all day to check repeatedly. Even at one A.M., Creed knew the fat man wouldn't be able to wait until he got home.

The engineer lived in an apartment over the studio, and as the door slowly hissed shut on its closer, Creed heard him say, "Make sure you spring the night latch when you leave, will you, Robbie?"

Inside, Robbie was left alone in the control room's dimmed light. There were no messages, and he sighed, replaced the receiver, and closed his date book.

The parking lot was nasty, there was a lot of fog, and his car was sitting in the middle of a small lake.

"Dang."

Creed squeezed the trigger . . .

"Jerry? You at a place you can stop? The car's loaded."

"Yup. Perfect timing. Thirty seconds, and I'm a free man until Monday."

. . . as Robbie squeezed the Volkswagen's door handle.

Robbie felt the force of a well-swung lead pipe hit

him in the face. He snapped over backward and came down on his back in the puddle, gasping for breath.

Lungs were the first organ to shut down, and the panic of slow suffocation leaped into his throat and streaked down the spines of his arms.

There was little pain, just a coarse smarting between his eyes where the bullet had entered. It felt like a pimple that was being squeezed—hard— refusing to break.

His heart shut down in a violent melodrama, fluttering, thumping twice with the bursting force of a large drum.

Flit—trapped moth.

Fight—a third thump.

Flop—old friend, impeccably reliable since many months before birth. It felt like the miraculous organ was skipping beats, the intensity amplified a thousand times.

Fourth thump—stillness.

Additional terror and panic stung the singer like a surprise slap from a large, angry woman. Then the gray miasma of drizzling night blended into the gray blood spots before his eyes. The fat man fought desperately to keep seeing, but the scene quietly faded as if on a dining-room rheostat. Body Glorious was totally immovable, paralyzed. The last few fragments of Robbie Lyn Gilson's mind scuffed around inside of his head, and he wanted to cry very badly. He wanted to blubber, run to Mom. He wanted to pee—but he couldn't move. His final sensation of life on earth was barely perceptible; it was the evaporating coolness of the mud puddle on his cheek.

He was too dead to feel the lifting, dragging; pants pulled down; first pointed, sharp prick . . .

"Daddy?"

"Okay. I'm done. Yahoo! The last one in the water when we get there is a rotting monkey carcass."

"Yckk."

CHAPTER THREE

"How much longer, Daddy?"

"We're almost there, sweetie. Last one in the water is a . . . a . . ."

"A rotten monkey carcass!"

"Noooo. Something nicer. A well-fluffed purple kittie."

"She hears a whole lot more than you think she does, Jerry."

"I suppose."

"You've been awfully quiet. Are you working on the book?"

"Yeah. I'm trying to work out a slipup for Chapter Five. He's got to make a mistake. So far the cops haven't got anything to go on. This one's such a departure from *Kingdom*. I can write horror; but mystery—police procedure . . ." He let the sentence hang.

"By the way, Pashun Pit called this morning. They want you for a six o'clock on Tuesday to sing backup on some jingles."

"Damn. I was planning to write on Tuesday. It'll take all day Monday to get that air conditioner fixed. I was hoping Larry would help me some. I guess I'd better be thankful. Sessions are hard enough to come by."

She was silent.

"Did they say who was doing the lead vocals?"

"No. Tobey said there were three jingles to sing for the group. He didn't say who was doing the lead, just that they're doing tracks all day; backup vocals are at six."

"Shit!"

"What's wrong?"

"Well, if it's going to take all day to cut tracks, then there've got to be horns and strings on them. Why the hell didn't they call me to arrange?"

"Well, it's their loss, Jerry. I think he said Peacock was doing it. They usually have their own arrangers, don't they?"

"Shit. I'll bet pus-brain Minsterketter's gonna do it. He couldn't arrange to die if a tank shot him."

"I wish you'd watch your language. You just saw how Ginger picks up on every thing you say. I have to wrestle with her over her language. She's only six."

"That's your problem, Lauren."

"I'm making it your problem, Buster!"

"I'm sorry. Let's not get into a fight. This is sup-

32

posed to be a fun weekend. God knows I need a little fun."

"Well, get your head out of that damn book and pay some attention to your family for a while. Have some fun for a change."

"Yes, Maam. Watch your damn language."

They both grinned without looking at each other.

The car pulled onto the red sand road that led down a steep ridge for half a mile to Kentucky Lake. A sign said, "CAYCE'S CADENZA."

Middle July was unusually hot and had had more than it's usual scanty allotment of rain. The woods were thick and luscious, and ripe blackberries loaded the bushes beside the road. Lauren made a mental note to pick some of them to take back to Larry. Larry was her twin brother and a consulting engineer for several race-car manufacturers. He was totally addicted to two things—speed and berries. It was not unusual to open the freezer compartment of his refrigerator and find it packed with dozens of packages of frozen berries—strawberries, raspberries, blueberries, blackberries. One of his favorite meals was chocolate milk and peanut butter–raspberry sandwiches. She shivered mentally at the thought. Also, to ride with him was enough to turn dark hair to white. He seemed only vaguely acquainted with an automobile going less than seventy miles an hour.

The cottage smelled musty, as usual. She went about opening curtains and exclaiming while Jerry unloaded the car. The air conditioner would make short work of the smell.

The place could hardly be called a cottage. There were five bedrooms—four upstairs, including the large master that led out onto a deck over-looking the lake. A giant family room dominated the downstairs, open for two stories to the vaulted ceiling-roof.

The summer home had originally belonged to Jerry's grandfather, who had lived out of state. He had fallen in love with Kentucky Lake on a fishing trip. Jerry had inherited it when his widowed mother had died.

It took him about five minutes to unload the car. There had been a brief time-out while he tied Ginger's dancing life jacket and raced the wild giggles to the dock. She had worn her bathing suit on the trip. He always managed to let her jump in the water just before he did. Today, still in his clothes, he started to stop short, but thinking better of it, hooted and jumped in, clothes and all.

By the time the wet musician had finished un-loading the supplies, Lauren had changed from her white cotton dress into a string bikini with a matching hairband. His groin fluttered, as usual.

He had never got used to having a wife who was

34

nothing less than stunning. Her hair was naturally blonde, long and bushy; eyes were a deep and unusually dark shade of hazel; lips were just enough oversized to promote a musky sensuousness; and a smattering of freckles on her cheekbones served to force a kind of all-American-beauty that stopped conversations and snapped heads wherever she went. She had also kept her perfectly proportioned figure since the day he'd met her. The scar of a six-inch slash across her stomach was the only blemish on otherwise flawless skin. But, alas, in stocking feet, she was an inch and a half taller than he was. In contrast, Jerry's five-foot-seven frame was soft and twenty pounds overweight.

He walked up behind her as she was arranging some fresh flowers. Hands slid around the skin of her waist and palmed her scar on her belly. He said, "I think that you are amazingly beautiful."

As he pressed and rubbed against the thin patch of cloth on her bottom, she cried, "And you're soaking wet, Buster!" Through Jerry's wet clothes, she could feel that he was beginning to think she was very beautiful.

She turned with a smile and ran her fingers into thick red curls that framed a cherubic rosy and freckled face. Lips and nose were a size and a half too large, and mahogany eyes were just a little too close together. The total effect was not unpleasant, but it would never get him tagged as hand-some.

Looking down at the front of his pants and making several scratches at the bulge, she whispered, "My, my. Aren't we a horny little bugger this morning?"

Scuse me — bruise me — use me — bay - beh — Aa-owwww —

he sang softly, in a scratchy rock style. It was one of a number of voices he'd developed over the years. Jerry was one of the talented few who could convincingly sing the lead part on a jingle or blend with the backup singers on jingles or albums. A close-quarters, arm-pumping, leg-flopping dance accompanied the music as he scrunched his eyes, backed off a little, and did a fake left, go right, spin.

She caught him, continued the spin, heading him toward the door, and slapped him on the wet rear end. No longer whispering, she said, "Lunch will be ready in a while, Casanova. Go check the boat."

"I'm gonna go check the boat now, bay-beh," he sang as he continued the dance, strumming an imaginary guitar, hopping one-foot à la Tom Cruise in *Risky Business* and allowing the momentum to carry him through the door. Outside, still dancing, still singing, he stripped off the wet

T-shirt and sneakers and hung them on the back-porch pegs reserved for wet swimming suits. The dancing and singing finally died a natural death.

Two mockingbirds about fifty yards apart were giving recitals as the musician walked down the path to the boathouse. They would repeat each phrase two, three, sometimes four times, then segue to the next composition. The birds could go like that for an hour and never repeat.

"Hi, Daddy. Come on in!"

Ginger was paddling around in the shallows as Jerry reached the boathouse.

"Maybe in a while, honey. I gotta check the boat first."

The sixty-five-foot houseboat rocked gently inside the oversized boathouse. He climbed aboard, turned off the alarm, and entered the salon. The large room was decorated in white and pastel green. Furniture and lamps were in a soft yellow bamboo motif. In addition to the salon, there was a galley the size of a large kitchen and three state-rooms the size of most bedrooms.

For the last three years, the boat and cottage had received considerable use. After fifteen years of working in the recording industry as a player, a singer, an arranger, and a producer, the constant arrival of younger, more contemporary musicians, most of whom were also computer whizzes, had caused Jerry's arranging and playing sessions to slowly, but surely, dwindle. There were a couple of jingle accounts that he still produced, and there was still some singing, but work was only a fraction of what it had been ten or fifteen years before. He struggled to keep up with the styles and technology, but there was an overwhelming flood of musicians who ate, drank, and slept one specialty or another. Gone were the days when one man could cover all the styles by using raw talent and an acoustic piano. It hurt desperately to see accounts he'd kept for years go to younger musicians who were as at ease piling up exquisite sounds on an electronic keyboard as they were programming a sequencer slaved to a high-end Macintosh computer. He'd even overheard someone refer to him as a dinosaur one time. Fortunately, with Lauren's geriatric counseling practice and his inheritance, money wasn't a problem.

So, in his free time, he'd started writing a novel. As a songwriter, he had a feel for words, and ever since he was a kid he'd had a fertile imagination, conjuring up monsters, cowboys, space creatures. The hard part had been finding a publisher. It had taken him eight months to write the first book and almost two years to find a publisher. The novel was set in the horror genre—demons, blood, kinky sex, gore, and it had done more than moderately well. Publishers usually expected to lose money on a first book, but *Kingdom Mine* had surprised them. It had made good money. They were anxious for the second book. Maybe after this one, he'd quit the music business and write full time.

Saturday afternoon they went a long way down the lake in the houseboat, taking turns pulling Ginger and each other on the inner tube. Evening came and they found a secluded cove, fished, swam, ate, and drank. Lauren had brought the makings of a Mexican feast, and by the bottom of the first blender of margaritas, everything was very funny. Ginger was put to bed, and the second blender led to discarded swimming suits and a skinny-dip. Jerry tried repeatedly to make love to Lauren in the water, but too much alcohol wouldn't allow him to perform. He grumbled, "The Mexicans have hatched a diabolical torture here, woman. Special, secret ingredients in margaritas are designed to greatly increase the desire for lechery but prohibit any performance."

Lauren corrected him. "That was Shakespeare, you sod!"

"Shakespeare was a Mexican?"

He continued the love efforts in the shower and bed, but finally gave up only after vowing to continue in the morning. It had happened many times like this through their years of marriage. He'd get drunk, couldn't perform, and they'd put it off until morning. By morning, Lauren was never in the mood, no matter how horny he was. In fact, Lauren was rarely in the mood. Even before they had been married, he'd known how complex she was and that she would never want sex with him the way he did with her. But he'd accepted the trade-off of having such a beautiful woman for a wife, a woman who'd wanted kids and who'd been a good mother. Quietly, he'd sublimated his drives into hobbies and music, and hoped that one day she would change.

After lunch they weighed anchor, and Jerry pointed the houseboat in the direction of the cottage. This part of the lake was complicated with islands and gravel bars. The shoreline was uneven and periodically gave rise to long back bays. It was a stretch of water where it paid to remain between the buoys.

The family was on the flybridge. Lauren was enjoying the scenery, Ginger was coloring in a color book. Jerry was deep in thought, his hands not even on the wheel. There was an old, deep-sided fishing boat in front of them about three hundred yards. Both boats were cruising about the same speed. Jerry was snapped back into consciousness as a black jet boat came careening into the channel from behind one of the islands. It must have been doing ninety. It just appeared, aimed right at the runabout.

In the space of three seconds, it blasted into the side of the fishing boat and leaped high into the air. The two men in the runabout were catapulted over thirty feet from the boat. Both landed limply and began to sink without a struggle. The aluminum runabout had been folded in half from the impact, and it too began to sink. The jet came back down on the water, bounced a couple of times, and continued as if nothing had ever happened.

Jerry jumped to his feet and screamed, shaking his fist while the other arm reached for the throttles to jam them all the way forward. The boat leaped under full power. Ginger and coloring book fell off the chair with a loud "Shit!" Neither of the men in the fishing boat had been wearing life jackets. He had to get them. Maybe he could dive and find them—revive them.

Lauren jumped to her feet and hollered, "Jerry, what's wrong? What is it?"

He turned quickly to her to see why she hadn't seen the horrible accident. Pointing frantically, he screamed, "Didn't you see? . . . What the hell . . . What?" His eyes jerked back to the water ahead in the channel.

"Jerry, what is it? What happened?"

He looked at her in total confusion, then back to the water ahead.

"Didn't you? Wha . . ."

"There's nothing there—just that little boat. Are you going into one of your lost-time episodes? Are the little green men going to beam you up to their flying saucer? What did you think you saw?"

Jerry ignored her cheap shot and said, "Lauren, if I were going into a blackout, neither one of us would know it, would we?" He looked directly at her and said, "And it's not my fault that your stupid doctor friends can't find anything."

He had been enduring the blackouts for a year now. There'd been half a dozen doctors, and Vanderbilt Hospital had kept him for three days, shoving needles in him, taking EEGs, EKGs, CAT-scanning every millimeter of his brain. About once every three of four weeks, he would wake up, usually at home and in bed, remembering nothing for the last several hours. One time, he had lost a whole day. Lauren maintained that he had acted perfectly normal the whole time, but try as he would, he could not remember. The doctors never had come up with a solid explanation. She remained silent.

They were now long past the island where the jet had appeared. The fishing boat was still ahead of him, but only about a hundred yards. The men were in it—without their life jackets—and the long inlet had appeared on the port where they could see the outline of the cottage and boathouse at the far end.

Shaking his head, he was completely confused. It had been absolutely real even to the detail of the cap rocking slowly on the waves as the jet made its getaway.

He throttled back and turned into the cove.

"Damn! I must be cracking up!"

Ginger retrieved her coloring book with another, "Shit!"

CHAPTER FOUR

Summer after-Sunday-dinner sun filtered into the old barn's oft. Loose hay was piled mattress-high in the corner to make a bed. She lay waiting on a faded patchwork quilt they had dug out of the attic. After he'd climbed the ladder and slowly shuffled across the floor with embarrassment, she said, "Switch places. You lie here. I want to make this good for you."

He took her place on the quilt as she stood and began to sing to herself slowly, softly:

> "Jesus Loves the Little Children
> All the children of the world . . ."

Eyes cast downward, she continued to hum the song while she slow danced for him. Then seductively she unzipped her jeans and wiggled them to the floor. She was wearing nothing underneath, and the unfurred furrow boasted its preadolescent innocence. His breath caught at the sight, and as the shirt came over her head, he saw tiny transparent nipples harden on undeveloped breasts. She went to him, lay beside him, and they kissed. For the two ten-year-olds, it was a long, slow, openmouthed act of love.

I

Creed covered the singer's body with a tarp weighted with four cement blocks. In the back of the pickup, it was inconspicuous, especially at one-thirty in the morning. When he got back to the house, he hitched the jet boat to the truck and transferred the bundle and the blocks to the boat. He also took his fishing pole and tackle box from the garage and put them in the boat. He wanted to be able to justify his presence on the lake at that hour of the morning. Not many jets went tooling around Kentucky Lake in the middle of the night or, at best, early dawn. If confronted, he was doing a little fishing.

The two-fisted pile of meat had been carefully wrapped in wax paper after he'd disected it in the woods. Damn, he had enjoyed that. As it had with the derelict under the bridge—the practice run—the whole scene unfolded over and over. He squeezed the head-snapping trigger, plunged the knife, and with both hands offered Robbie The Asshole's asshole to the invisible cloud bellies above the trees. He had worked desperately to hold back the guffaws of laughter that threatened to split his head wide open in the middle of a silent woods filled with fog and rain. It was a whole lot better than the best drugs.

With the tremendous amount of adrenaline that was flowing, he knew he wouldn't be able to sleep for at least two days, maybe three.

"Might as well go ahead and baptize Robbie now."

He would retire the derelict's body from the shallow grave in the swamp near Shelby Park, too. Even as well as it was hidden, there was always a chance. The lake was a much better idea, and the body had only been buried a few days. Get rid of both of them. Eliminate all opportunities for mistakes. Every second the bodies weren't at the bottom of the lake was an opportunity to get caught.

This time he'd planned from the beginning to sink the body in sixty feet of water in Kentucky Lake—a long way from the scene of the crime—in a remote backwater—on a soft, muddy bottom that would cocoon it quickly. The bottom of the Cumberland, which ran through Nashville, was clay. A towboat with barges could jar it loose. Besides, the Cumberland rarely got deeper than thirty-five feet, most of it sounding under twenty-five. Even wrapped in chains, there was always the chance that an anchor could hook the bundle or pry loose a disintegrating hand or leg.

He could spend the rest of the day reliving the

high—at one hundred miles an hour and a couple of six-packs, some uppers. Damn, it'd be great.

He found another small box in the pantry and another Magic Marker in the desk. Just like the first time, there was no sense labeling it until the last possible minute. If he were stopped for any reason, the first question the cop would have is, "What's in the box labeled 'Police,' buddy?"

He parked the truck, this time with the boat and trailer, in a dark spot in the lot of the Quality Court Inn across the bridge from the Justice Center. It had been absolutely fortuitous when he'd remembered the old cleaning company shirt. A dimly remembered acquaintance had left it at the house after an all-night drinking spree and had never come back to claim it. The man was as big as Creed, and the shirt fit just fine. He put the shirt on over his T-shirt and started for the bridge. At three o'clock in the morning the streets were steamy and deserted. The red "L & C" from the top of the Life and Casualty Building glowered at him as did its reflection in the river. Before selling out, the insurance company had made much of its fortune selling "industrial" policies to the ignorant and the poor—high premiums for the low coverage—excellent salesmanship—sometimes selling as many as ten policies to the same person.

Once inside the front door of the Justice Center, Creed quickly scratched Police on the box, wiped the Magic Marker of prints, and threw it in a wastebasket. Using surgical gloves, he had repackaged Robbie's rectum in fresh wax paper and cleaned the box with alcohol to make sure there were no prints on it.

He was even luckier this time. There wasn't anyone in sight at the front desk. He placed the package off to one side of the desk, hoping it wouldn't be noticed until later in the day. No one saw him come or go.

II

The rain clouds had exhausted themselves and given way to small patches of stars when Chris Taggert stopped the truck at the apex of the horseshoe driveway in front of Frankie Suboda's trailer. Chris blew the horn and scratched a two-day beard on skin the color and texture of a grocery sack that had been wadded up. The trailer was surrounded by piles of junk washers, air conditioners, TVs, rusty cars, and unidentified pieces of machinery. An engine block had suffered death by hanging as it dangled from a tree branch on a block and tackle.

Frankie appeared in the doorway, then waddled down the path. His John Deere cap had enough grease on it to service a truck. For a month Chris had watched a split elongate in the side of the buldging overalls. A lobe of white blubber squeezed through like the Pillsbury Doughboy.

Frankie heaved himself into the truck with several

airy grunts and a long, fractured fart. Chris ignored it, as usual, and Frankie gave the door a teeth-jittering slam. The engine started reluctantly, the cranky pickup finished the driveway and pulled slowly onto the bumpy dirty road. Chris never drove over forty even on a good road. He would go forty-five if events beyond his control forced him onto the interstate.

"Rain must a stopped one, two o'clock. Road's 'most dry. Supposed to be hot agin." Chris would do all the talking. Frankie was never up to it at this hour.

The dirt road changed counties and turned to coarse blacktop that was well punctuated with potholes.

"News said water's surface is eighty-five. Too hot for fish. Too damn hot."

No-passing lines were introduced when the blacktop changed townships and most of the potholes disappeared in favor of a finer and darker mix.

A contorted mile rolled by. The road was following a ridge.

"See the Daniels kid went on to his re-ward Wednesday night—'bout ten. Wrapped th' C'maro around a telyphone pole—old Delary Road. Knew he'd gid it. Hell, they's still a eighth-inch'a rubber out front a Greeley's where he peeled out last week. Steve said they bought three six-packs."

Frankie tipped the pint of Thunderbird that had magically appeared. There was another one in his back pocket when this one was gone. There was also a case of Blatz in a large cooler in the boat.

The truck turned onto the dirt road that led to the lake.

"Great Goud, they's been a lot of rain. Garden's done half drownt. Doubt if I e'en get t'maters outta it."

Dawn was sloshing its alpenglow over the eastern ridge when Chris shut off the motor at the first crappie hole. Silhouetted trees formed complicated black filigrees against the early light. The boat rocked gently in the silence, twenty feet from a small spit of land that was populated with thick woods and brush. On the other side of the point there were some ten-foot shale cliffs that dropped into deep water. The quiet was polluted by a distant roar that crescendoed with a Doppler effect as it came toward them.

"Goddog jet! What the hell's he doin' out here this time a mornin'? What a racket!"

The noise kept coming until it reached the other side of the point. They could hear the boat surf on its own sizzling wake as the engine was slowed to an idle pop, and then cut off.

In the fresh quiet, two mockingbirds resumed their interrupted vocal duel. They were about fifty yards apart in the woods, and their calls came in well-panned stereo. Chris was operating the electric trolling motor, crawling the boat along the bank. Neither man said anything. He piloted the runabout clear of the point to reveal the jet, and there it was, about seventy yards away, rocking furiously in the water's mirror of dawn. There was one man in it, and he was wrestling a long, and what had to be heavy, bundle over the side. He didn't see the fishermen until it splashed, and he raised his attention to see if there was by some remote chance anyone within hearing distance. The surprise on his face turned to loathing, and he quickly started the jet and rocketed away. The ridge of trees that dawn was still skulking behind marched the disgusting roar down the river, and the echoes gradually decrescendoed with the distance.

"Wonder what the hell that was all about."

"In a hurry."

"Guess we'll never know. There's sixty feet of water over there."

"Shit. S'go over t' Stumpbottom. Be bitin' over there."

Chris started the eighteen-horse Johnson, and they headed across the lake. It would take about fifteen minutes.

III

Creed couldn't believe it when he looked up and saw two men watching his every move. He had rewrapped both bodies in the tarp and tied cement blocks to the bundle with chains. How much could they see? Could they tell what it was?

He had no choice but to hightail it out of there. As the minutes passed, he became more and more furious. By the end of four minutes he was boiling, and the jet's speedometer was registering one hundred even. A one hundred foot rooster tail sprayed gloriously from the transom.

There was only one thing to do. He didn't have a gun with him. He'd left the .22 hidden inside a wall back at the house and forgotten to bring another weapon with him.

"God damn, why didn't I bring something. Anything. Even a fucking pistol. I could have wasted them easy. So help me God, nobody'll catch me again without some kind of weapon!"

He turned the boat around, then opened it up again still seething. He was actually shaking all over, he was so angry. There could be no loose ends—this was life and death, not some kid game of peeking in the windows. Those men could comfortably put him in the electric chair, and that was definitely not in the chart.

They couldn't get very far in ten minutes.

IV

Chris and Frankie were almost to Stumpbottom, a long, shallow backwater dotted with thousands of stumps.

Chris had throttled the motor back to just above

an idle and was slowly threading the boat between several islands.

He shouted above the motor, "The only thing that feller coulda been dumpin was a body, Frankie. Why else'd he come way out here at this time a the mornin'?"

Frankie's brown voice loudly proposed, "Nukeer waste?"

"Hell no. They got good places for that. My guess is it was a body. Probably some dope dealer. That's what I'd do if I wanted to git rid a one. Dump it in sixty feet a water with ce-ment blocks. I think I saw a ce-ment block. You see a ce-ment block, Frankie?"

"Jesus!"

That was all Frankie could say. He never got a chance to answer the question.

Out from behind the island came the jet— screaming! It headed right for them, unswerving.

Chris froze for two seconds then instinctively tried to turn the boat away, but it was too late. The fishing boat had been moving too slowly for there to be a significant response from the little outboard's rudder, and the jet was just too blistering fast. Neither man was mentally ginger enough to jump overboard and avoid the collision. The jet hit the fishing boat broadside and flew over the top. It's chines hit the men with the impact of a hit-and-run automobile at one hundred miles an hour, and both men were dead before they were thrown into the air. The jet's bullet-proof Kevlar hull was barely scratched.

Creed slowed and turned back toward the fast-sinking aluminum boat. There was plenty of flotsam and jetsam, but the only trace of the men was a John Deere cap rocking on the waves.

The big man floored the throttle and raced dawn, once more topped off with adrenaline.

"Hey, little guy."

"Larry! How long you been standing there?"

"Oh, just a minute or two. Hotter than the pizza oven room in Lower Hell in here." Larry, blond hair, blue eyes, tall, tanned, and handsome was leaning against the jamb of the attic door grinning at Jerry.

Jerry made a copy of his working disk on the old Tandy 1000 SX, then locked both the original and the copy inside his desk drawer. He could easily afford a new, hard drive computer, but steadfastly refused to buy one until the Tandy gave up the ghost.

"Man, I appreciate your helping me with the AC. I hate to pay some greedy jerk three hundred and fifty dollars for something I can do myself. What time is it anyway?"

"About three. The new compressor's in the truck. Shouldn't take very long." Larry originally had said he'd be out of town until the next day. An hour before, he'd called to say he was back early and would drop by to help.

Three hours later, they were sipping Heinekens

from frosted mugs in a well-cooled den while Lauren worked on supper's lamb chops and steamed vegetables in the kitchen.

Larry was always helpful—more than willing to take time off from work when he was needed, but Jerry found he had to watch for his own safety. Lauren's twin was a klutz—the most careless man the musician had ever known. He was always dropping something on Jerry's foot or beaning him with a swinging board or falling ladder. Today he'd dropped the compressor as the men pulled it out of the back of the truck. Had the one-hundred-pound unit landed on Jerry's foot, which he barely managed to pull out of the way in time, it would have put him in the hospital.

Lauren had called immediately—within the space of one minute—to ask if everything was okay and would lamb chops be all right for supper. Jerry wondered if the twins were doing their thing again.

The phrase "Be a lert. Nashville needs more lerts" had popped into his head. It had been written on the wall of the john at the musician's union. Jerry had been alert for nearly twelve years, and he had every intention of continuing to sleep with one eye open.

CHAPTER FIVE

I

"Honey, have you seen my date book?

"It was on the telephone stand a few minutes ago."

"There it is. I looked right at it."

"Jerry?"

"Yeah, hon."

"Ginger's in the front yard. I forgot to give her a Flintstone. Before I forget again, will you give her one on your way out?"

"Sure."

"What time will you be back? Do you know?"

"No. It'll be late. We may have to go all night. The stuff's got to be mixed and on the ten A.M. flight to L-A-X. The client wants them for a two o'clock meeting."

"Okay. I've got a late meeting with Sam Bruckstein to compare some notes, but I'll be home probably no later than ten. I won't wait up for you."

"No, don't. I may not be here until noon. Especially if Charlie's in a celebrating mood in the morning. It's going to mean a pile to him. Say hi to Sam for me. It's been awhile since I've seen him." Sam Bruckstein was a psychiatrist. Jerry knew the real reason Lauren had a meeting with Sam.

"Sure. See you later."

The thought of stroking Fat Charlie Barkley's obese butt in order to keep the account was revolting. Like eating pickles and mustard on strawberry ice cream. The man was a politician, not a musician. Jerry deserved this account, not Fat Charlie. If an opportunity with the client raised it's ugly head and it was an absolute certainty that Jerry could get the account, he might have to tell the client that the product and the ad agency were getting shortchanged. They deserved better. In the last year, Jerry had done some things he never would have thought possible to acquire and keep accounts. Things like "Yeah, great voice, but the cat sings out of tune—takes all day to get the group on tape if he's singing in it—expensive at two hundred dollars an hour." "Yeah, Marty's a Florida State boy, I think. Nice guy. Too bad they were short on good-arranging teachers when he went to school down there." There were other things—things said, things done that Jerry didn't want to think about. Fortunately, he'd been smart enough, so far, not to get caught. He was still known as a jolly and harmless has-been around town.

Lauren opened the downstairs bathroom door and came out rubbing her hands with Vaseline Intensive Care.

"You know in all these years, I still haven't adjusted to you being out all night. How come all you drug-crazed musicians are such night owls?"

"Well, it certainly doesn't happen as much as it used to. I suppose I could always start a new career—maybe a bank teller—or cabdriver. Pretzel bending! Gotta be good job security in bendin'. We could start a little mud slide on the side. Combine it with a ladies' lingerie boutique. You could answer the phone, 'Cayce's Mud Slide, Custom Pretzel Bending, and Ladies' Lingerie.' "

"That's a good idea. I'll see you when you get here."

"Man's unending battle for the dollar is unending."

"For sure. Here is Ginger's vitamin."

As Lauren entered the kitchen, she could just barely hear Ginger's "I don't want that shit" and Jerry's "Sweetie, this shit is going to make you grow up to be a big shit just like Mommy and Daddy."

"Why me, Lord?" she asked, as she started running water to scour the breakfast frying pan.

II

Jerry sat at a worktable in the recording studio's repair room. He had shoved several tools, a voltage meter, and a hodgepodge of electronic bits and pieces aside to make a space. He wrote in longhand on a yellow legal pad.

"Hey Farley."

"Yeah, Jeeters." Jeeters had a cup of coffee in each hand. It saved a trip.

"Front desk got another box early this morning. Said when you came in, to tell you to come down and get it. They didn't dare open it for fear of screwing up evidence."

"Does it look like another present from our anal retentive friend?"

"How the hell should I know. They just said, tell you to come get it."

"Great."

Farley shuffled a stack of papers and laid them off to one side of his desk so that when he returned, he could place the box on a level plane. He drudged through the office door and took the elevator to the ground floor.

"Farley. Just the man I wanted to see. Hey, we got a bet goin' down here—if this really is another asshole?"

Farley saw the box and moaned, "Oh, no!"

The box's size and the word "POLICE" printed in black letters were identical to the last one.

"The bet's this: I bet Barlow ten bucks that you can get your fist through it. He says you can't get a fist in one, you know? Like when the procto tests you for prostate, he has to stick his hand in with the fingers extended. I say they got good stretch—like a woman's pussy. You know—at birth?"

Farley looked at him in fatigued unbelief, unsure if he was being put on or not.

"You lend it to us so we can see—when you're finished?"

"Take it from me, Georgie, your fist oughta fit. We know for a fact that your head will."

"Ah, c'mon, Joe. A bet's a bet."

"You didn't get your grimy little fingers on it did you?"

"Ayyye, what's a good cop for?"

Farley pushed the two blue bulletin-board tacks he'd brought with him in opposite corners, picked up the box carefully, and walked across the lobby. He brushed the elevator button with a little finger and slumped against the wall with a shoulder. He was tired and certainly not looking forward to confronting what was probably inside.

His hair had started graying only during the last year, and he wasn't sure if the dark brown had been polluted by worry and late nights, or just the family genes. At least the late nights were no longer an excuse for a fight. It had been two years since his wife had left him—after twenty-four years of marriage and two grown sons. She said she'd fallen in love with another man—one who would be around once in a while and who wasn't likely to get shot.

Back at the desk he sat and stared at the unopened box with dread to the dismay of the hastily assembled audience. The word had spread. With not a little prompting, the detective finally donned his rimless shooting-style bifocals and began his examination of the box. He hated the glasses, but he just couldn't see anything up close without them anymore.

Jeeters pulled a chair up beside the desk and asked, "Where'd we get it?"

Farley answered, "It just appeared again on one of the booking desks in the front lobby."

"You look tired, Joe."

"Yeah. It was a long night."

The afternoon before, the department had received a call from a Vanderbilt biology student who had been studying the metacercaria of a tapeworm found in raccoons. He had been working in a swamp upriver from Shelby Park and had run across a strange hole. He said it was the right size for a grave and had been recently dug up. There were what appeared to be some not-too-old bloodstains on the surrounding leaves. He figured the police department—

"Hey, Jerry."

"Back here, Pat."

"We got the drums up. You ready to start playing Mr. Pro-du-sor?"

"Hoday dokay, Joe! Ret's make many how-so praybacks."

"You be de produ-cor today, not de produ-cee, baby. Dat's goo, Momma."

"I be de main man. You be de chickenplucka. We tapdance goo' on de client's haid."

All of the dialogue had taken place without either man really taking part in it. It was automatic pitter-patter to ease into the high-powered intensity that could have everybody on Cloud Nine before the day was over, or have everybody at each other's throats.

"What are you scribbling, Jerry? Still working on the new book?"

"Yeah. Sometimes I get brainstorms, and I need to get them on paper or I forget them."

"I forget you're gettin' old."

"Not so old that I can't make you . . . bend . . . over!" Jerry made a feint at the engineer's balls. The man doubled over to protect himself, then made the same feint back. They both laughed.

"I jiss love grabassin'. Don't chew, sssweetie?"

"Oo la la, say Pierre."

The jingles were being produced for a Chevrolet dealer in West Virginia. The ad agency rep would be arriving in half an hour. Hopefully, he wouldn't have the Chevy dealer with him. That usually turned into slow-mo disaster. Rarely did a client know enough about music and recording technology to make reasonable requests. Jerry always made the stipulation that if the client came to the studio, any extra studio time would be tacked on. It would not come out of the original budget.

"Other pickers ready?"

"Yut."

The building for this particular studio was on two levels. The downstairs housed the repair room, where Jerry was writing, along with a kitchenette and a small midi studio. There were also several offices that belonged to publishing and production companies. The two men went up the stairs and down a hall that led to the studio itself. A doorway opened from one side of the hall to reveal a lounge, complete with the coffee, snack, and bottled water machines found tucked away somewhere in most studios. A doorway opposite led up one step into the control booth where a cacophony of guitar and keyboard licks poured from the speakers.

The thick, soundproof door was propped open, and the men entered an almost silent large room where three seated rhythm players were creating all the noise that was coming from the control room. Synthesizer, bass, and guitar were all feeding directly into the "board" and the only sound in the room was a soft unamplified plinking coming from the strings of the bass and electric guitar.

Along one wall were three more doors that led

to isolation booths. The middle door was open, and Jerry could see the skeleton of the electronic drum set and its four-foot stack of black boxes that belonged to the drummer. The drummer usually arrived half an hour early, hoping the cartage company had brought, and set up, his equipment. If the man was playing actual drums instead of beaters and pads that electronically triggered a computer, it usually took half an hour to balance and equalize the seven microphones on the drums. Today it was electronic. There were no drums in the room. From a floppy disk, the drummer could trigger over ten thousand drum sounds including the actual sampled drums of hundreds of drummers ranging from Phil Collins to Buddy Rich.

"Hey Pat." Jerry walked over and closed the door to save the drummer the trouble of getting up and threading his way through the maze of stands, cymbals, and computer equipment to do it himself. Isolating the drummer was habit more than anything. There were no microphones on the other instruments to bleed into. Everything went directly to tape via computers.

"Yo, Jerry." The drummer waved a stick at the arranger as the door was closing, ignoring the useless act.

The guitar player's "ax" was connected to three square feet of foot-pedal switches that were plugged into a three-foot stack of black boxes that could drastically alter and doctor the sound.

They keyboard player was triggering from an old Yamaha DX7 FD synthesizer which had over ten thousand sounds available for it on floppy disks. These could be combined, two at a time, with a midi computer that stored one hundred twenty-eight sounds. Using a Macintosh computer, a player could combine the DX, a stack of three or four midis, another synthesizer like a Roland or a Korg, and their midis, and gigantic never-before-heard sonifications could be generated in combinations of up to sixty-four at one time. It was the musician's ability to continually astound the field with new sounds that kept him in demand for records and jingles, sometimes at triple scale.

The bass player was running his electric bass through his own "stack" to enhance and purify the sound. He informed the engineer that only one of his earphones was working, and the engineer quickly replaced them with another pair. "Still out. Must be the box." The engineer then replaced the small box that the phones plugged into. The player replied, "Ay-Oh-Kay. Thank you and good night," and the engineer left the room for the control room.

The piles of black boxes, gadgets, and hundreds of feet of wire running across the studio floor were a grim reminder that hi-tech had gobbled the music industry whole.

Jerry handed each musician his part and put on a set of phones himself. He would run the arrangement down once or twice in the studio before returning to the control booth to record.

Two hours later, he was back at the workbench writing on the legal pad again.

. . . might be more than a little interested.

Farley had been up the entire night with the forensics squad taking samples by arc light. Nobody wanted to wait until daybreak. If the blood turned out to be human, they wanted to know about it as quickly as possible. A trail could be getting cold.

The bacteriology runs would probably be the most helpful. He'd thought of calling the forensic entomologist from Memphis, but the body had been buried. Looking for blowfly eggs that had been scraped or fallen off would be needle-in-a-haystack hopeless.

When the preliminary results came back from the lab, there was no doubt: It was a grave—robbed! The blood belonged to Homo sapiens. It had been concentrated with pieces of brain matter where the head must have rested. In the area of the buttocks, there was more blood and a little striated muscle tissue.

The lab men also found some lint samples from the victim's clothing. They were covered with layers of sweat, grime, and dirt and had to belong to someone who hadn't had a bath in a long time—a vagrant? A lot of them slept on the banks of the river. Nearer town, there was a whole village of shacks and camp-sites.

Farley had only been to bed for three hours the preceding night. He had been questioning the street people, some of whom were only seen at night. It was going to be difficult to establish if someone was missing because these people had made a career out of being lost. Most of them didn't want to be found. Some even thought their way of life was glamorous because they were dependent on nobody for anything. An alcoholic could go on a binge in Nashville and wake up in Little Rock five days later having made his way without even knowing how.

"Hey, Jerry. You in there?"

"Ahyut."

"We're ready to go. Strings are all set up."

"Be there in a second, Bobby."

He continued writing.

There was no reason to believe that the grave belonged to the assholeless victim. It could have belonged to anybody. But the cop's nose and the blood-stains at the point of the buttocks' resting place, told him it did. The obvious question was why the hell had the body been removed? If the grave had only been temporary, what had the killer been waiting for?

* * *

"Jerry? We're ready. Are you here yet?" The engineer called loudly down the stairs from the control room.

Jerry once more left his writing. As he came through the door to the booth, he replied, "I'm here. I'm here. I was just over there, now I'm here."

The ten string players were visible through the large double-glass window. Six violins, two violas, and two cellos, they were practicing various runs in the music, warming up.

Jerry walked to the board and pressed the talkback button, which allowed him to talk to them through their phones. He said, "Hey gang." They stopped playing. And turned to face him through the glass. Jerry continued, "Wanna know the definition of a minor second?" Without waiting, he said, "Two violas playing unison." The five men and five women players grinned at him, including the viola players. Viola jokes were the current rage in town. They knew Jerry meant only fun.

"Gotcha." To the engineer and the strings, he repeated the old Smothers Brothers line, " 'Hit it, Riddle!' Ya got eight ticky-tickies between the ears." The engineer started the twenty-four track machine that played the tape with the morning's rhythm section already on it. The drummer's eight beats of click count-off were heard, followed by a half-bar drum kick, and the string sweep came in exactly the way the arranger had heard it in his head when he'd notated it on the score paper. By the time the track had reached the jingle's bed, the section of music where the announcer would read the sales pitch, Jerry's mind was busy working in another studio.

CHAPTER SIX

I

Creed walked in the studio door at exactly two o'clock. Most of the eleven other singers were already back from lunch, and they had been there for the morning sessions from the signs of the Styrofoam coffee cups and junk-food wrappers. One of the sopranos was on another diet. She had a gallon jug of water she would sip from throughout the afternoon. Creed had seen her go through the routine of pigging out, then dieting furiously after she'd ballooned fifteen pounds.

The diet factor speared his head like an arrow. He was at least forty pounds overweight himself and horribly out of shape. For the last three years, he'd rationalized that the extra weight made him a better singer—it added depth and texture to his voice.

His face started to swell and sweat when he realized that they'd done a ten-o'clock session without him. It was embarrassing to be called in as a substitute. With Brother Robbie Gilson out of the way, things should have started to pick up by now. Maybe he'd have to knock off another one. The cops would catch on though—if it were too soon. HEADLINE: "Where are all the bass singers?"

He said hello to the contractor and silently called him a cocksucker as they shook hands. The swelling and sweating on his face raced down his neck and out his shoulders. It was no fun being a second-class citizen. "You bastard. You'll get yours. Why the hell didn't you call me for this morning?"

"Who's arranging?"

The contractor, a little embarrassed at the fact that it was obvious that Creed knew by now he was only a sub for someone who couldn't make the two o'clock session, answered, "Tommy Dishane. He asked for specific people, Ron. Sorry. He's been working with the same group for years."

You liar. That is simply not true. I won't lick your dick, that's all. How the hell did Dishane get the project in the first place. He couldn't arrange to wipe the shit that came out his own asshole.

"Hey, Ron, are you working next Tuesday at ten and two?"

Ron opened up his date book and tried to hide a white week.

"Nope. What have you got?"

"Gorman's doing a Christmas project for RCA. Dishane is arranging. It'll be at the Shed. Gorman always used Robbie, but nobody's been able to find Robbie for a week—not even his girlfriend. I'd like to use you."

"A ten and a two on Tuesday, the fourteenth, at the Shed. Thanks, Terry. Progress, dammit. Gorman's been using Fatso Gilson for years. Nobody is ever going to find Robbie, my friend, except the fishies at the bottom of Kentucky Lake.

"How come John is using Tommy to arrange? He always uses Bob Trane, doesn't he?"

The contractor answered, "I don't know. Tommy says he's been awfully busy. He's even had to turn down some stuff. After that hit with Crystal Gayle, he's gotten real busy."

"Good for Tommy." The son of a bitch didn't call me to do the stuff he couldn't handle. Goddamn it, I can write with anybody in this fuckin' town. I'm the best string arranger in Nashville. Why won't they let me work. The bastards are jealous, that's why. This singing shit is for the birds.

"Okay, kiddies, let's make beautiful music. Make me rich." From inside the control room, the producer keyed the external speakers on the wall over the glass window. "Welcome aboard, Ron."

"Thanks, John. It's nice to be here." Creed gave the producer his best second-class-citizen smile as he put on his earphones. He caught the ". . . be here" in the live cue.

"You're gonna get yours, asshole" was only inside his head.

II

"Lauren, I'm gone."

"Wait a minute" came on a low shout from the kitchen. "I need the checkbook. I've decided to abscond with the plumber."

"Cute."

"It's in your glove box."

Jerry never had been exactly sure why Lauren had married him. There had been a raft of guys with Corvettes and Porsches fawning after her in college. The only time he'd ever been given an answer as to why she'd picked him, she'd simply replied, "Jerry, I've dated those kinds of guys. They're selfish, they lie, cheat. You see them fooling around on their wives no matter where you go. I want a man who really loves me—a guy I can trust beyond a shadow of a doubt. A man like that will be the father of my children." Jerry already had known that she wanted children badly. She had made that plain. The female complications with Ginger had prevented her from ever having any more, and the disappointment had never really left her.

Lauren came into the hall from the kitchen, wiping her hands on a dish towel. She was wearing an oversized T-shirt that had a picture of a saxophone and a cymbal on it. The caption read SAX CYMBAL." Jerry had found it in a music store in Memphis years before.

"Your group session still on tomorrow night?" They went through the front door and across the porch toward the driveway. With her doctorate in thanatological counseling, Lauren led several group therapy sessions a week for people with terminal illnesses and for others with loved ones who were terminally ill. The largest group met on Saturday evenings, and was comprised of the latter.

"Of course," she answered. "You ask me that every weekend, and I give you the same answer." She draped the towel over the porch railing.

"Well, I'm waiting for a Saturday night you're off so I can take you out on a real date. You know? Like other people do on the weekend—wine, dine, get supine—then I ravage you at will."

"Jerry, those people need me. The loss of a loved one is not dealt with so easily by some. For several of those people, the pain is the most traumatic thing they've experienced in their entire lives."

"Probably just as well. I happen to know for a fact that Saturday night is your kinky night anyway."

"What?" She turned to him in surprise.

"Don't look at me in disbelief. Before you started that ridiculous group, I remember many Friday nights when we made the beast with two backs. The hood and all that black studded leather? Of course, first you had to do your little tricks with the whip. Oh, yes, *the whip*! Did that ever smart! Then there was that big revolving torture wheel; and the block-and-tackle system; and the sandpaper-lined thumbcuffs. Kinkier than a washtub full of snakes, Lauren. Don't deny it. I never could figure out why it was just on Saturday nights though."

An abashed smile remained while she shook her head in disbelief at where her husband's fervent imagination took him sometimes. Lauren had always been just the opposite of kinky. The times when she didn't have a headache or was too tired, he could hardly get her out of the missionary position.

"Dream on, buster. Maybe you need to be in a therapy session." The smile finally dissolved, and she asked, "What time will you be home?"

"Well, I'm sorry to say, it's going to be late again. Carruthirds likes to work all night. He's a night owl. He's also a chintzy son of a bitch—he gets the studio a lot cheaper from ten P.M. until ten A.M.—and on Saturday. I'm the fourth arranger he's gone through, and if I want to keep the account, I have to lose the sleep. I'd rather be with you" be said as he put his arms around her. "Last weekend at the lake was great." He smothered the "great" with a more-than-juicy kiss, and Lauren didn't pull away.

"Are you two smoochin?" They were standing next to Jerry's car.

"Ginger, Daddy's going to work. You get to kiss him good-bye." Jerry kissed her again.

"Time! Time! My turn." She jumped up and down, blond pigtails dancing

"I thought you were next door with Jennifer."

"She was being a shit today so I came home."

Lauren released Jerry and ordered, "Ginger, don't say shit! Kiss Daddy good-bye."

"Bet I can kiss juicier than you can, Mommy."

Jerry hoisted his daughter to lip level, and she kissed him in a perfect imitation of what she'd just witnessed, complete with her hand running through his hair the way she'd seen on "Days of Our Lives."

She finally let go, and Jerry gave a flabbergasted "Wawh" as he put her down and got in the car.

"See, Mommy?"

"I see, honey. You're going to be breaking hearts before you're seven."

Jerry handed her the checkbook through the window.

Lauren took it, matched his good-bye, and headed toward an appointment with the vacuum cleaner.

III

Lauren was thirty-seven, seven years younger than Jerry. They'd met at a party after a dance when she was in her fourth year of graduate school. He was playing and singing in a well-known regional band, and much to his surprise, when he asked her for a date she'd accepted.

For that first date Jerry had borrowed a canoe, and Colonel Sanders had packed his favorite picnic lunch. They put the canoe, padded with rolled-up blankets, on the top of his BMW and made the ninety-minute trip to Barkley Lake Resort. Jerry got the canoe off the car, and they filled it with life jackets, paddles, coolers, picnic paraphernalia, and cameras. It turned out to be a lot heavier than it should have been, and Jerry struggled at the rear end as they carried it fifty yards across the park's lawn to the water. Three times he asked if she'd like to put it down and rest. Three times she said no, she was fine. Pride would not let Jerry put it down, and he finally arrived at the water's edge with a hyperextended elbow and a pulled shoulder muscle. Lauren hadn't even worked up a sweat. The perfectly proportioned limbs bore much stronger muscles than would ever be expected. Her strength still amazed him on occasion.

A year later, they were married.

IV

It was there. He knew it would be. The trap had worked perfectly. For several nights the fat old male had been scavenging scrap on the lawn that the boy had left closer and closer to the trap. The animal looked at him with tiny myopic black eyes. Getting it out was only a little difficult. Strapping it up by the hind legs was harder.

"I guess one less possum in West Texas isn't going to make much difference. You seem to be losing the game on the roads anyway. Damn, you are stupid!"

She was lying on her bed when he started to skin the animal alive. In her mind she felt his ecstasy, knew the animal's exquisite pain. She winced when the knife slipped and slashed him across the finger. The next morning when she awakened, much to her surprise, she found that she had the same sore wound.

V

Creed put the gun case behind the pickup's seat and climbed in. Fortune had indeed smiled on him. When he'd called Tommy Dishane's answering machine from the pay phone, the arranger's wife had answered. Creed had given her a fictitious name and said he needed to talk with Tommy about some sessions next week. She said he was mixing at Pond Creek from six until ... It would be all right to call him.

Pond Creek—it was too good to be true. It was as isolated as Pinewood—and the quicksand ... This was a chance too good to pass up. And there was a full moon!

He wasn't going to use the gun on Tommy. Tommy's curtain would ring down a littler slower. Creed wanted to watch the lights go out. Dishane did not deserve to be working the way he was. He was a dickhead—more politician than musician. He'd never written an original lick in his life. The only reason the producers didn't catch on, was that most of his arranging was for strings, and it was practically impossible to make strings sound bad, regardless of what you wrote.

With the asshole Dishane out of the way some of that work would have to come to Creed. He had waited long enough. Enough dues had been paid. He deserved to work more.

The studio layout was familiar. He'd worked there a few times. There was a long hall off the back door, and a window looked into the booth. Another window looked into the studio. It was absolutely perfect. He could see everything in the building, and no one would ever know he was there.

He entered the hall at exactly ten o'clock with no

weapons. If someone discovered him, he'd say he was supposed to be there for a ten-o'clock sessions, and after checking his date book, he'd find, with great surprise, that he was at the wrong studio. Through the windows he could see Tommy and the engineer. There was no one else. He left unseen, went to the truck, which he'd parked down the road, and drove a few hundred yards to a dirt road. He switched off the lights and after driving a hundred feet in the moonlight, wheeled into a short path blocked by a pasture gate. He got out, opened the gate, and drove into the pasture. After turning the truck around, he cut the engine and started out on foot for the studio. He was careful to close the gate. The truck was invisible, cut off from view by a thick hedgerow that bordered the road.

He checked the Browning .22 automatic pistol to make sure a round was chambered and the silencer was tight. This time he'd dumdummed the bullets. If he had to use it, it'd be from short range and only because the engineer had come out the door and discovered what he was doing to the asshole Dishane. Two bodies were as easy to dispose of as one. He'd already proved that.

Creed was six-three, and with forty pounds of extra weight, he weighed in at two hundred fifty—more than enough to handle five-foot, seven-inch, one hundred thirty-pound Dishane.

Plastered with insect repellent, the big man sat

down in front of a tree on the border of the parking lot about ten feet from Dishane's 240 Z.

It was only forty-five minutes later when he saw the door open and heard the arranger saying good-bye to the engineer. Creed quickly got up and closed the ten feet, ducking low behind the car.

". . . Her . . . morning and book it. You're sure?"

The engineer was too far into the building for Creed to hear the response. His pulse quickened and the diarrhea urge built in his bowels. He opened the can of ether he'd bought in a Louisville hardware store and soaked the dish towel with it.

Tommy came directly to his car, which was backed into the slot. He opened the door and was just start-ing to get in, when Creed smothered his face with the dish towel. Tommy struggled briefly, but Creed held him until he relaxed totally, dropping the keys. The big man picked them up and dragged the arran-ger around the car. He opened the passenger door and dumped the limp body into the passenger seat.

This time he would have to dispose of the car. Two disappearances of musicians with their cars left in the parking lot would send flags. He'd got away with it with Fatso Gilson. Gilson's car was always breaking down anyway. The cops would think he'd got a ride with a stranger and—Ta ta, Robbie.

This car would go into the quicksand—no trace. The deadly ooze was part of an extensive swamp that briefly touched the bottom edge of the field where Creed's pickup was parked. He'd hunted the area several times, and each time, the owner had carefully warned and reminded him about the quicksand. It was just another indication of how perfect a setup this whole thing was.

Driving the car down the field's slope by the light of the moon was easy. The field was fairly smooth. It had been pasture until several cows had been lost, in spite of elaborate fencing. There was a steep hummock overlooking one of the quicksand pits at the bottom, and Creed lined up the Datsun for its last trip and killed the engine. Then he dragged the unconscious Tommy Dishane thirty yards to the stand of oak trees that lined the field's border. He taped Tommy's mouth, stripped off the little arranger's jeans and underwear, and strapped him very tightly to one of the trees, face-to, standing up. A broken ammonia capsule brought him back to a thoroughly confusing consciousness.

Tommy screamed until he was gasping for breath through a nose not designed to gulp air. Except for his head, he found he could not budge an inch. Wrist-to-wrist, and ankle-to-ankle, his arms and feet were tied together and stretched excruciatingly tight around the tree's circumference. Bark pricked his skin in a hundred places. Terror of the known and unknown flooded every cell in his body. He couldn't see, he couldn't speak or move, and he could hardly breath. When Creed shined the flashlight on the side of his face, the skin was the color of cooked ham.

"Well, Tommy. Here we are again—you with your touchhole hanging out in the wind."

"MMnninnmmm."

"It's okay. You don't need to thank me for what I'm about to do."

"Hhhmmmnnnnmmmooomm."

"I know, I know. It'll sting a little. But it's all for your own good, Tommy. Now listen carefully: I am about to make the asshole's asshole just a teeny bit larger than what it is already. That way you will be able to get into the *Guinness Book of World Records* for not only being, but also owning the largest defecation device in the whole goddamn world! And at absolutely no cost to you or your Blue Cross!"

Creed played the muffled screams for a while with the point of the knife. Finally, unable to hold back any longer, he drove the eight-inch blade in to the hilt and twisted it back and forth.

Tommy stiffened and shuddered violently. He had flattened against the tree so hard that blood trickled freely down his chest and stomach to join the torrent flowing down the inside and back of his legs.

Then the big man withdrew the knife and began the serious cutting.

CHAPTER SEVEN

Jerry could not tell when he was in a blackout. Neither could Lauren. Life went on with total normalcy. He worked, joked, attending to daily demands, and things only became confusing when he awakened from a nap or a night's sleep having no recollection of the past few hours or the previous day's afternoon and evening. No matter how many questions he asked, and no matter how hard he wracked his brain, the memories remained encased in tons of well-seasoned cement. The periods were always ended by waking up; he had never just popped out of one to wonder, "How'd I get here?" Sometimes he lost as many as twelve hours, and for all he knew, he could have machine-gunned an entire elementary school or flown to Siberia and back in a jet fighter.

When the blackouts had first begun, he had asked a lot of questions about the stories of people being allegedly abducted by aliens and having no recollection of the event or the lost time until placed under hypnosis. After the fifth or sixth episode, he discarded the idea that aliens were beaming him up and wiping his memory. "No alien would go through the process that many times just to study this body or empty this feeble little brain." He finally told Lauren what was happening to him. She had been of little more help other than to suggest a battery of tests at the hospital.

The shock and terror slowly turned to delight the first time he'd gone to the attic after breakfast to discover the computer still on, the screen covered with words, pages, hours of work. He read the story with utter fascination—a first-time reader. As he scrolled through the pages, he wondered, in awe, where the medical terms had come from—terms Jerry Cayce couldn't ever remember seeing, much less using. He flinched at the horror of the deeds, marveled at Farley's homespun philosophy, and admired the characters for their wit and ingenuity. The plot unfolded effortlessly before him as he read . . .

"This one's really been mutilated, Farley. It's the old twist-the-knife trick." Sanger looked a little pale, in spite of his years of conditioning.

"God Almighty that would hurt."

"Yup. And the victim was alive when it was being done, too."

"Erythema." Farley spoke it as a fact, not as a question.

Sanger donned only part of his lecture voice and said, "Yes. The blood was circulating around the wounds just fine." He pointed with a probe, but Farley had looked away. "Observe here and here, severe edema. Traumatic infraction."

Farley refused. He'd seen enough.

Sanger continued, "It's our Rambo Reamer again, too. From the width of some of these cuts, I'd say it's a big knife and it was in about as far as it'd go."

Studying the back of his hand, the detective didn't comment, so Sanger filled in with, "There was one of those horror movies one time—Nazis or something—lowered this guy on a three-foot spike—up the bum—then bounced him."

Farley finally looked at him in amazement and said, "Sanger, you're one of the most morbid guys I know."

Sanger brightened noticeably and said, "Thanks. Every little bit helps."

The distraction allowed the detective to finally look down at the piece of meat briefly. He said, "Well, we know our friend wanted to torture this one. He must have either really hated the guy, or it's just his way of letting off steam."

"One less customer to buy B.V.D.s, that's for sure."

Farley came back into the office in time to catch Jeeters pouring the second bag of Folgers into the fluted filter. There was another unopened bag in front of him that would quickly follow.

"Jeeters, from now on, we want triple donations from you for the coffee fund."

"Aw, come on, Farley. With just one bag, it tastes like diarrhetic ape scats. You know that as well as I do. It's just their way of selling more coffee. You're supposed to put in at least two bags."

"Triple, Jeeters, or knock it back to one bag."

The routine had been going on for three years now. Jeeters wouldn't pay any more, and he would continue to put three bags in the machine as long as he wasn't caught. He put the third bag back in the drawer and returned to his desk to await the brewing coffee.

Farley looked up from what he was doing long enough to say, "Any luck running down the boxes?"

"No. All three box manufacturers said it's a standard. They make thousands of them every month. Ship them all over the country."

"What about the Magic Marker found in the wastebasket?"

"No prints. We couldn't trace it. It was just a standard Magic Marker, black. Too many of them sold in every Tom, Dick, and Harry store in Nashville."

"I knew that. But we had to try."

"There's a couple missing persons reports on your desk. Could be connected to the asshole case."

"There *are* a couple, Jitters. 'Are' goes with the plural 'reports.' You don't say, 'There is reports on your desk,' do you?"

"Who gives a shit."

The men on the force who knew Farley, respected his detecting skills with an almost religious awe. He had made a reputation nationally after putting away a federal senator for the murder of a young blackmailing mother who had borne the senator's illegitimate child. The case had read like an Agatha Christie murder, and the best-seller and television movie had only fanned the fame. He'd donated the money they'd paid him for his part to the Policemen's Benevolent Fund.

But when it came to fair-game potshots, Farley was treated like everyone else. He liked it that way and usually gave better than he took.

"Jitters, how many kids've you got? Two ... three, aren't there?"

"Three. Three girls."

"Do you know what the difference is between your daughters getting a forty-thousand-dollar-a-year husband, or an eight-thousand-dollar-a-year husband who's gonna always be on welfare?"

"Why do I feel you're gonna tell me?" Resigning himself to one of Farley's lectures, Jeeters took out his handcuffs and began to polish them with a special rag he kept in his desk. Jeeters had a fetish about polishing his custom-made chrome-plated cuffs.

"There are three things that make a difference in whether a girl has class or not, Jitters. Class!"

"Like you, Joe—class."

Farley took out his handkerchief, looked intently at it, blew with a great honk, and looked intently at it again. "Listen and save yourself a lot of grief."

"I can't wait."

"Number one: Teach those girls to speak the King's English. A woman can go anywhere and be comfortable if she can articulate the language correctly." Farley made an upward tossing motion with his fingers to emphasize the word "articulate."

"Number one: King's English."

"Number two: Make sure they learn a foreign language—preferably French. French adds intrigue, romance, to a woman. You never can be sure what a woman's thinking if she can speak French fluently."

"Okay, two: French fluently. I can hear the old family cash register ringing already."

"Number three: Make her learn to play the piano. That's the kicker, Jitters. A woman who can play Chopin can pick and choose any husband she wants."

"After ... articulating the language correctly," Farley had been speaking with only half his mind as if on automatic pilot. He had glanced at the first report on his desk and seen that Tommy Dishane had not come home after work three nights ago. Tommy's wife said that the arranger was a stable, dependable husband, not given to taking off without telling anyone where he was going. Farley scratched down her phone number and address in his notebook and, after finishing the harangue on Jeeters, began to read the details.

At ten after one, the string players had signed the card, packed their instruments, and were leaving the studio. Farley had watched and listened from the small anteroom with the video games, kitchen sink, and coffeemaker. When the players had all left, he opened the thick door into the control room and stuck his head in the door.

"Can I help you?"

The engineer was tipped back in his chair, feet on the leather-padded edge of the console. There were two other men with long hair and beards sitting on a long vinyl sofa. A fourth was packing a large sample bag with music scores and parts.

Farley showed him his badge and said, "Farley. I called?"

"Yeah," the engineer answered. "I'm Bobbie Thamesley. You wanted to talk about Tommy."

Farley had gone to Dishane's house and talked for over half an hour with his wife. He had come to the conclusion that either Dishane had her completely buffaloed, or she was telling the truth. The arranger was making good money, he loved what he was doing, he was a doting husband and had two gorgeous little girls who would be extremely difficult to leave if the urge came upon him to pull up stakes and desert.

"Tommy's a good boy, Inspector. He works hard and pays attention to his family. He adores those two little girls."

"He just left the other night? Nothing unusual?"

"Yeah. What more can I say? He was going to call the office in the morning and book the room a couple of days next week."

"He never called?"

"Nope. I asked Lorraine—the secretary. Tommy's very dependable. If he said he'd call in the morning, then he would. I saw him write a note to himself in his date book."

"A devoted family man?"

"Yeah. You don't even need to hint about that. There wasn't anybody else. Some men really do love their wives. It's not all like on television."

"Ever had any trouble around here at night? It is in the boondocks."

"Only one time. A guy got mugged in the parking lot. Kind of unusual for the country."

"They catch him?"

"The fool made off on foot. Some dopehead."

"Another musician?"

"No, he was not a musician. Most of the studio musicians are not dopers, Inspector. A lot of us are stand-up professionals just like doctors and lawyers. God knows we study as long as they do to master our trade."

"Sorry. I deserved that. What happened?"

"Well, the muggee gave the mugger a hard time. The dopehead got the worst of it, dropped his hat, and ran off down the creek. We called the sheriff, and a deputy was here in ten minutes with a dog. Said he just happened to be on this side of the county, and his dog usually rode with him at night. Anyway, the dog trailed the doper about a mile. The idiot tried to cross a swamp and got stuck in the quicksand."

"Quicksand?"

"Yeah. The pond out back is fed by a creek that drains a large swamp. There are some bad patches of quicksand in it."

"Can you give me the names of some of Tommy Dishane's friends?"

Thamesley did, and Farley wrote them down.

"Enemies?"

"I doubt if he had any. Not that I know of. He was a good arranger and well liked. I hope he's okay."

"Thanks. I appreciate your time."

Farley got in his car and headed back toward town. Outloud, he said to himself, "These are Missing Persons' problems—not Homicide. What the hell am I doing wasting my time?"

There were three other murder files waiting on his desk along with one more missing person report. Two of the murders were family affairs—cut and dried. The other was probably drug related. He picked them up, one by one, and began reading.

The next day, when he would finally glance at the missing person report filed by Robbie Gilson's girlfriend, he would begin to think he might have been wrong.

CHAPTER EIGHT

I

Jerry came in the kitchen door from the garage workshop and wrapped his arms around Lauren as she stood at the sink scraping carrots. He lifted her ponytail and began kissing the back of her neck.

She shivered and said, "Hey stranger, fooling around with my husband's wife?"

"There's a whole lot more where this is coming from, baby. You know you want it, and I'm the guy with the sugar stick to put in your bowl."

"Oh, I want it, but you don't have the guts, stranger. My husband would make mincemeat out of you."

He began undoing her jeans.

"Aahhh! Jerry! Ginger and Jennifer are in the playroom. They might come barging in here any minute. Let me see if I can get them to go next door and play."

He let her go, grabbed his crotch, and began hollering, "Cock alert! Cock alert!"

Ginger walked into the kitchen and was trailed by the six-year-old who lived across the street.

"What's a cockaler, Daddy?"

"Let's see you get out of this one, Casanova."

"Hi, sweetie. What are you two up to?"

"What's a cockaler, Daddy?"

"It's a big bird, honey. Why?"

Ignoring the deflecting question, she continued, "What were you grabbing at your pants for, Daddy?"

"For a while, Ginger. Just for a while. Why don't you and Jennifer go over to her house and play for a while."

Ginger had her mother's freckles and blond hair. Today the hair was braided into one thick pigtail. Her father's brown eyes squinted a puzzled look across her face, but having come to the conclusion that he was not going to give her any interesting answers, she turned to Jennifer and said, "Parents are so zasprating in manure sometimes. Come on, Jennifer. Let's go to your house."

When the door had shut behind them, "Nice job, Cassie. Let me finish these carrots."

Jerry got a beer out of the refrigerator, popped it, and took a long guzzle.

"What are you doing in the workshop, Jerry?" She put the carrot sticks into a plastic, container, covered it, and dried her hands.

"Oh, just dinking around. Have you seen that

can of liquid rubber we used to make the Halloween masks with? I've looked all over for it."

She turned and looked at him with a strange expression, "What in the world do you want with that?"

Before he could answer, she went on, "Jerry, you were up all night, it's two o'clock on Saturday afternoon—rest period. Maybe you should take a nap—lie down."

"Let's go upstairs . . ."

"All right. I would love . . ."

". . . To the hall closet."

". . . A nap—the closet? That ought to be interesting."

On the way up the stairs, he explained, "Stupid *Wide World of Sports* has got another winner on today—There's a contest to see who can run up the mountain, and then, by God, down the mountain the fastest. Riveting. The Braves aren't on either. TV on Saturday afternoon is the trots anymore."

"What *are* you doing in the garage?"

They stood in the hall before the open closet door.

"I was going to make a mask for Ginger," he answered, unbuttoning and unzipping her jeans.

"Getting ready for Halloween a little early, aren't we?"

"Oh, I don't know. I just had a stupid urge," he

replied, pulling the shirt over her head. She wasn't wearing a bra.

"We've never done it in here before."

"Do you want me to get some of the toys?" he asked as he pulled off her jeans. She wasn't wearing panties either.

"No, I think we can manage without them."

The phone rang as Jerry began to strip.

"Oh, dear."

"Gotta be Larry. Get rid of him, please."

Lauren's twin had a nasty habit of calling whenever they were about to make love, which wasn't often. Lauren walked naked into the bedroom to answer, leaving the musician standing in the hall by himself.

Most of what Jerry could hear was Lauren's okays and yeses. She finished with, "I'll call you back in a while."

"Was it?"

"Of course."

"What'd he want?"

"He said there was a sale on at Kastner. He's redecorating his living room and wanted to know if I'd go with him to pick out some things." Larry lived alone in a condo on Old Hickory Lake. Although he dated some, he had never married. He seemed more interested in cars and boats than in women.

"How wonderful."

At least he had used the phone. Lauren's relationship to her twin had always been more than a little spooky. Over the years, Jerry had never adjusted to his wife being able to communicate with her brother without talking.

Some of the titillation had disappeared, but the couple managed to take up where they had left off, stepping into the closet naked to close the door with giggles.

II

Sunday morning Jerry slept late. When he had finished with his toilet and come down the stairs, he could smell the Swedish pancakes and sausage Lauren was making. Sunday morning Swedish pancakes were a ritual in the Cayce household. Lauren's grandparents had both immigrated from Sweden. Ginger was already at work on the first one. It was smothered with spiced applesauce.

"Oh, that smells good," he said, sniffing with exaggeration. "You Swedes sure know how to do some things very well."

On the way to the mailbox to get the Sunday paper, Jerry was overwhelmed with the smell of mashed flesh. It had rained the night before and hundreds of frogs and earthworms had sacrificed themselves on the blacktop for a few moments of warmth provided by the previous day's sun soaking into the road. Because his home was situated on one of the higher elevations, he could see the tree-carpeted hills of Nashville stretching before him in a one-hundred-eighty-degree swath. The Cumberland River ran through the center of the city, but there was very little river valley. Most of Tennessee's capital rose and fell on an endless parade of heights that defied any hint of sameness or boredom.

He retrieved the Sunday paper and would spend an hour in the recliner devouring it from front to back, including all the advertising pamphlets and coupon giveaways. He had only been reading for five minutes when he raised his voice loud enough to be heard over the running water in the kitchen.

"Hey, Honey?"

She turned the water off and answered, "Yeah?"

"It says here that missing person reports have been filed on two musicians."

"Who are they?"

"One is Bennie Stein—he's an arranger—you've met him."

"Yeah."

"The other is Rory Pinnerton."

"I don't know him."

"He's a reasonably good bass singer. Okay arranger. I think he produces a couple of jingle accounts. I played keyboards for him one time when he got stuck."

"Does it say anything else?"

"No. The last time they were seen was at late-night sessions."

"Where were the sessions?"

"One was at Boondocks, the other at Gideons."

"Those are both out in the country, aren't they?" She walked into the den carrying a wet green pepper. There was another strange look on her face.

"Yeah. They sure are."

Something was beginning to dawn on Jerry's mind that he didn't like the feeling of at all. In the last two weeks, his novel had included murders taking place at two isolated studios. A bass singer and an arranger had been murdered by the stroke of his pen. *My God, what a coincidence. I can't believe this.*

"You don't have any sessions at those places, do you?"

"No. I haven't been to either in a long time."

The phone rang, and Lauren went back into the kitchen to answer it. She picked up the receiver and Jerry heard her say, "Hi, Michael. How's the cop business going." There was the usual exchange of clichés, and Lauren finally said, "Yup. He's right here." She called, "Jerry pick up. Michael wants to talk to you."

"Okay. Thanks."

Michael Farbur was the guitar player in one of the country bands in which Jerry had played keyboards a number of years before—until he'd got too busy arranging and producing. Now that the work had died off, Jerry would have welcomed the chance to play with the band again. Unfortunately, his replacement was well entrenched. Occasionally, they would call if the new piano player couldn't make it. Michael was a Metro cop—another frustrated amateur musician who would gladly kill to be able to play music for a living but would never be good enough.

Jerry picked up the phone and said, "Hi, Mike."

Michael answered, "Hey, ya ole ivory whacker, we need a keyboard player for a rehearsal tonight—play a little, listen to some of the new tunes, and take chord charts. You wanna sit in?"

"Sure," Jerry answered. "Let me ask Lauren if she's got plans for me."

He covered the receiver, and was about to ask the question when she hollered from the kitchen, *"You can go outside for a while if you're a good boy and eat all your peas!"*

"Okay," he said into the receiver.

Jerry asked what time the rehearsal would start and what kind of beer to bring. He was looking forward to playing with the guys, but the anticipated fun was overshadowed by the coincidence of the murders in his book and the disappearances of the two musicians.

III

The band rehearsed every Sunday evening in Michael's living room, much to the chagrin of his wife, Toni. The musicians played, sang, and drank from seven to nine or as long as the beer held out.

The rehearsal began like it always did with the usual current dirty jokes, tuning, and warm-up licks. Jerry had brought his Roland D-50 synthesizer and plugged it into the PA amp. The band played a couple of old standards that Jerry had played with them for years, then started on some of the newer country hits.

The rehearsal ended when Michael was in the progress of putting a new Travis Tritt single on the turntable. He said nonchalantly, "Hey you'll never guess what Homicide is working on right now."

"You mean the missing person stuff in the paper?"

Michael continued, "No. This stuff won't ever hit the paper. It's X-rated."

"What are you talking about?"

Michael went on, "We got another serial murderer in town. He cuts out the victim's asshole and sends it to the police station in a cardboard box."

Jerry turned white as a sheet and said, "I got to

go, guys." To the astonishment of the other three men, he packed the keyboard and left, countering the barrage of questions with a feeble, "I don't feel good. I think it may be the flu."

CHAPTER NINE

I

Jerry did not remember putting the Roland in the trunk and driving. He just drove. Once on the interstate, the next thing he remembered was seeing the exit sign for Bucksnort. The darkened interchange was over seventy miles from Nashville, and vandals had stolen all the state road signs to sell the aluminum.

He drove down the crossroad in a daze to find a place to relieve himself. There was the panicky feeling that his body was tumbling in slow motion in a huge vat of paste while at the same time his mind raced as inefficiently as spinning tires on glare ice. There was not the tiniest straw to grab onto that would explain these incredible coincidences. What scared him the most was within the last two weeks, he'd had two blackouts. Over six hours were missing, and he constantly had to suppress the feeling of raw and bloody terror that kept bobbing to the surface.

He was mulling the killer's choice-of-mutilation

coincidence over for the hundredth time, when his mind was snapped into focus by something that was horribly out of place.

"Jesus Christ! Oh, Jesus!"

He was on the wrong side of the interstate about to confront a whole line of traffic at a closing speed of one hundred thirty miles an hour.

To add insult to injury, Jerry woke up at six-thirty the next morning with no recollection of what had happened after leaving the rehearsal. He would never know about slamming on the brakes to spin around several times in the road. Amidst unheard curses, cars and semis miraculously dodged him to the left and right, some of them taking to the median and shoulders. He'd finally come to a stop on the side of the road facing the right direction. An hour later at forty-five miles an hour, he was still having periodical bouts of the shakes.

He awoke on his back and rolled over on his side. He couldn't stop the tears. The depression had descended slowly the way it usually did—first the airtight heavy blanket, then the vacuum pump sucking the life out of his very existence. The Prozac he took regularly did little but put a mask on it. The little arranger could feel an overwhelming and undefined anguish seething, churning in his chest. He wouldn't sob, but the tears soaked the pillow.

"My God, what is going on here? If I go to the police and tell them, they are going to slap me in jail so fast . . . Maybe those fellows are all right, and the asshole bit is just a coincidence. If I took the manuscript to the cops and showed them . . . The problem is, no one has seen it. I can't document when it was written. They'll say I killed those guys to cut down on my competition and wrote about it just for sensationalism. God knows why I mutilated them. If they were to find bodies in the cove across the lake from the cottage, I would have to be the killer. My God, the rest of my life in jail—or worse yet, in the nut house— away from my family, work."

Jerry was fairly certain that Lauren was still asleep. He would have a hard time explaining the tears. She had little sympathy for his depression.

They often had discussions about the book, but she had not read any of it—she wouldn't know. He was a little superstitious about anybody actually reading it before it was finished. It might put a hex on it—recompense for baring one's soul before its time.

Well, he was going to have to go to the cops or take the chance some more people were going to lose their center-cut hind ends.

No. He wouldn't go to the cops. There wasn't a snowball's chance in Hell they would believe he wasn't doing these things—he didn't even know himself. "When in doubt, wait. Maybe nothing will ever happen again. Maybe it's coincidence, and I'd be putting my head in the alligator's mouth. Wait and see."

II

During breakfast, the decision to go to the police was dumped upon him again—about as subtly as a well-thrown brick to the mouth.

Lauren had fixed him a bowl of Grape Nuts with sliced bananas. He had just unfolded the morning paper when "PRODUCER COMMITS SUICIDE," came into view in bold headlines on the front page. By the time he had read three lines, he was white as a sheet, had completely lost his appetite, and was on the verge of throwing up. The knowledge had thrown him into a fit of severe nausea and instant depression. The paper detailed how one of Jerry and Lauren's best friends had shot himself. A Music Row security guard had found him, had seen the light on at one-thirty A.M., and had investigated. The paper had probably lucked out and just got the story in under the deadline. It detailed a list of hits and artists the man had produced, including several national, currently running jingles Jerry had played and sung on.

The terribly squeezed and desperate "Oh, noooo.

Not again" got Lauren's attention, and when she saw how white he was—how utterly ill he looked, she came to him and instinctively felt his forehead with her hand.

"Jerry, what's wrong?"

He pointed to the article in the paper. She read.

"Oh, no. Not Franney. I just had lunch with Tina last week. She will be hysterical. It's senseless. He had everything to live for."

Jerry had covered her cool hand on his forehead with his own sweaty one. He was on the verge of tears as the nausea slowly ebbed from his throat.

His eyes were watery as he said, "Honey, sit down. I've got something to tell you."

The fifteen-minute explanation ended when he went to his briefcase, opened it, and handed her the several sheets of manuscript that were on top.

"This isn't even proofed yet. It's the very first draft. It was written yesterday afternoon between sessions."

III

It was late. Creed had been watching the new condo-office building for more than an hour. He sat in the truck about a hundred yards up the street. He'd been listening to a tape of the Singers Unlimited. They always put him in a good mood.

Fortune had once more smiled on him. He'd been driving down Music Row and had spotted Cocksucker Gorman, the hotshot producer, going in an office door. Creed knew it was where Gorman had his publishing company. At ten o'clock, there couldn't be too many people left in there.

At midnight, Gorman still hadn't come out. Creed got out of the truck and walked the entire perimeter of the building. Except for the producer's office, the whole building was dark. He went back to the truck and got the .38 Special he'd bought for twenty-five dollars from a dope dealer. He was sure the gun was stolen; the serial number had been filed off. He stuck it in his belt and covered it with his denim jacket. From a Baggy under the seat, he took the yellow dishwashing glove he'd worn while he'd fired the gun twice with his right hand several days before. When he'd taken the glove off, he'd deliberately turned it inside out. Now it was left-handed, and the inside was coated with the powder residual from the gun that would show up in the neutron-activation analysis. He had noted one time, when Gorman was making some changes on a lyric sheet, that the producer was left-handed.

The big man made a thorough check of the building to make sure it really was empty and then walked boldly into Gorman's outer office, closing the door. With a slightly raised voice, he said, "Hey John, Ron Creed here."

Gorman's inner office door was open, and he

called out. "Yeah, Big Ronnie. Kinda late." Creed walked into his view, and the producer continued, "What can I do for you at ... wow, twenty past midnight?"

"I saw your light on."

There were a couple dozen gold records hanging on the office walls along with a number of pictures of the producer with top-drawer celebrities and politicians.

Creed pretended to gawk his way to the producer's huge antique oak desk and finally said, "I was on my way home after a short ten o'clock. I wanted to ask you if they'd ... Damn! Grandpa John, What have you got in your hair?"

Gorman reached for his hair.

"No, here ..."

Creed walked around the right side of the desk, put his left hand out as if to reach for the thick black hair Gorman sported so vainly, and effectively blocked the producer's eyes as he pulled the .38 from his belt. He quickly placed it to the left side of the man's head and fired.

Blood and brain spray flew six feet to the wall and splattered as the body lurched sideways out of the chair to the floor as if to escape the blast.

"Bye, asshole. If they made bad records in Hell, you ought to feel right at home."

The big man opened the gun's cylinder and removed all six of the cartridges, one of them now empty, one by one. He had wiped them clean when he'd loaded the gun. He pressed the producer's right finger and thumb on the casings to get prints, then carefully placed the shells back in the gun. Next, he pulled the rubber glove onto the dead man's left hand, patting it down to seat the residual powder into the skin, then pulled the glove off and stuck it back in his jacket pocket. If the cops ran a neutron-activation analysis, they would believe that the dead man's hand had fired the gun. Finally, he wiped his own prints from the .38 with his handkerchief and then squeezed the barrel between the fingers and thumb of the dead man's right hand to print the barrel. He raised the left arm in the air and placed the gun in the left hand being careful to squeeze the fingers around the pistol's grip, the index finger to the trigger. More than one suicide had been ruled murder because, unknown to the murderer, the victim was left-handed and the murderer had set things up for a right-hander. Creed let the arm go limp, and the gun fell to the floor next to the still violently convulsing body. One of the kicking legs, rebelling at death, kicked over a wastebasket, sending it flying several feet across the room.

"Hey, you didn't need to kick the bucket, shitface. I mean, all I did was put a small hole in your pathetic pea brain."

He was sure Gorman was dead. There was a large hole in the right side of his head, and the producer certainly wasn't breathing. There had been numerous cases of people trying to commit suicide by shooting themselves in the head—and missing. The body could live with a good share of the brain blown away if the autonomic section remained intact. The victim would be a vegetable, but alive. This one was dead.

"Hot-wet fuck. I just love it when a plan comes together. Get the hell outa here, Big Bubba, and leave his asshole alone."

Creed went out the small inconspicuous side door and merged into the landscaped bushes. There wasn't a soul in sight as he made his way behind the house that had been converted to an office building next door.

The high hit him just as he made the Division Street entrance ramp to I-40. He played the scene over and over like a tit replay on a rented VCR movie.

He headed the truck toward Priest Lake. There was no way he could sleep. By God, he'd pick up a six pack and go skinny dipping.

The embullient scream would have been heard for several blocks had anyone been around.

IV

After Lauren had finished reading, her only comment was "Six-pack should be hyphenated."

Jerry was openmouthed flabbergasted.

"Don't you see what this means?"

"I don't see that it means much of anything, Jerry. Coincidences like this happen every day." She walked over to the sink and began loading dishes into the dishwasher.

Convinced that he would get not a whit of sympathy from his wife, the arranger began withdrawing inside himself. He would go over the coincidences on his own, surfeiting them with clear, cool logic. But inescapable was the feeling of the gun under his chin and the pull of his thumb on the trigger. It had never been more real.

V

Three weeks were clipped in the mostly empty date book before Jerry could bring himself to work on the novel again. His mind felt as if it were chiseled in stone. If it worked at all, it was in little ticks and clunks.

He'd hung around the house, watched TV, seeing nothing, and had spent a lot of time in bed. His fingernails were chewed to the quick—a habit he had never been able to shake when something was bothering him. There had been more than one occasion over the years when he'd finished a gig and the white keys on the piano would be covered with blood. He never felt the pain. The intenseness of making music far transcended the inconvenience of pain.

He lost fourteen pounds—that was one good thing that came out of all of it. *"Maybe I should have a few more life-threatening upheavals."*

On a Tuesday afternoon spur of the moment, he jumped in the car and made the forty-five-minute trip to Boondocks. The studio was in an isolated area about thirty miles west of Nashville. The engineer was there alone, and Jerry quizzed him about the disappearance of Bennie Stein. No one had a clue as to what had happened.

Jerry then drove back into town and then turned north on I24. He exited at Joelton and drove another ten minutes to another isolated part of the county. He had hoped to time his arrival so that the musicians would be on break if there was a session. There was, and Jerry was relieved to see that he knew several of the "pickers." Using the excuse that he was just in the neighborhood, he took the opportunity to casually ask about the disappearance of Rory Pinnerton. None of the men knew anything about it, and Jerry gradually worked his way into the control room and proceeded to quiz the engineer who was dubbing tracks onto a DAT tape. Again, his efforts were a total waste. No one had the faintest idea what could have happened to the bass singer who produced most of his jingle accounts at the studio. What made the disappearance all the worse was the fact that the man had a wife and two kids. The engineer told Jerry that the police had been there asking questions. Nothing. Rory Pinnerton had simply vanished.

Larry had called three times and asked Jerry to go to the horse races in Louisville, the car races in Talladega, and then the unlimited hydroplane races in Owensboro, Kentucky. It was uncharacteristic of Larry. The men had spent time together over the years, but neither was first choice as the other's best friend. Larry was persistent, and the fourth time he called, Jerry consented to go to the motorcycle drag races in Bowling Green. Larry seemed to enjoy himself, and although he quizzed Jerry about the book and the temporary trauma its author was experiencing, he was careful not to be distasteful. After the third Lowenbrau, Jerry loosened up enough to give a few answers that contained more than one syllable.

Lauren had been supportive and dead set against going to the police. However, after one week, she could see that this was more than just a passing bout with Jerry's chronic depression. He had fought the blues for years, sometimes with antidepressant drugs under the doctor's prescription, sometimes with alcohol. He had told her about the suicide thoughts. After they were married, he had even confided to her that he had attempted to kill himself when he was eighteen. His mother had found the empty sleeping pill container and called the ambulance. Another four hours and he'd have been dead.

"Jerry, they would say you're a nut. If they did anything, it'd be to have you committed. You are not capable of murdering a flea. Forget it. It's coincidence."

Jerry wasn't sure.

"But the blackouts . . ." He rubbed at a small swath on his neck that he'd missed shaving. It was annoying, but he didn't feel like getting the razor to fix it.

"Jerry, the last blackout you had, after the band rehearsal?—you were home, here, at nine o'clock. Ask Larry. He was here with me when you got home. It was the night someone stole his Lotus. Franney committed suicide. Probably he was in trouble somewhere. You know how he gambled. Maybe it was with the label in California—maybe they were going to fire him. We may never know. But I promise you that there's no way you could've killed him like in your book— You were here with me. He killed himself."

"But the mutilations the police got—the missing bass singer and arranger. Jeez, Lauren, that's taking the coincidence a little far, don't you think?"

"No, I do not. Sooner or later somebody was going to think of cutting out that significant part of the anatomy that he considered everyone in the whole world but himself to be. How many times have you called somebody you didn't like an asshole. Besides, serial killers have mutilated victims every other way. My God, that guy in Miami was cutting off his rape victims' little toes and sending them to Catholic priests! The girls were alive when he did it, too—and are still alive."

"I don't know. If I put any more murders in the book, and I've almost got to, in order to make it work—if any more people die—I'm going to have to go to the police."

"Okay, then we'll think about the police. Look, let me call Sam for you. He's a good friend and the best shrink in the city. I've known him since I was in high school, and I know I can get him to make a place for you, even if it's only for a while. I'll call Vanderbilt and see if I can catch him before he leaves for his office."

"Well, it'd be better than going to the cops. You're right—they'd have me in the loony bin within the hour." He paused a moment, then said with surprise, "Someone stole Larry's Lotus? Man! I don't remember that. Did he get it back?"

"Yes. A couple of kids took it joyriding. They found it in East Nashville miraculously unharmed." Larry had several sports cars. The racing Lotus was his pride and joy. The car would do in excess of 190 miles an hour. "By the way, you're not working tonight, and if you're not going to write, why don't you come to the therapy session. There should be about ten people there. It might do you good to see some people with real problems."

"No thanks. That'd just be taking coals to Newcastle. I've got some serious thinking to do. *Major realigning of my life would be more like it.*"

VI

For the next several hours Jerry didn't remember anything, although Lauren told him later that he was with her and perfectly normal the whole time. The blackouts were becoming more and more frequent.

As if to compound his problems, the next afternoon a girl ran into his Saab, while it was parked on the street—she totaled it; and the IRS sent a notice they were going to audit his 1993 tax return.

CHAPTER TEN

I

The big man was boiling mad but refused to show it. He would get the little cunt fart. He had her home address. He would get her and make her sorry she'd ever been born and lived sixteen whole fucking years on this planet. Because of a goddamn squirrel!

He had been driving through a residential section where they'd just finished overdubbing a small string section in a basement studio. Creed had done the arranging. There were a number of studios in Nashville that were converted basements, garages, family rooms. They were mostly used for demos, their rates being much lower than the regular studios.

Work was picking up. This call had been from a small, independent label that was cutting a new artist but didn't have much money. He'd also been called for several of fish-food Robbie's bass sessions.

The stupid twat had dodged a squirrel that had run into the road. She'd torn the front left fender right off the truck. Another couple of feet to the center, and she would have hit him head-on. And on top of that, she'd been drinking. *Jesus, sixteen years old and she's skunk drunk along with the other little bitch in the car with her.* Before the cop had got there, Creed had caught them dumping empty beer cans into the ditch.

"Hey, you can't dump those out like that!"

"Piss off, fatty. It's our word against yours."

"You'll get yours, missy."

A woman dressed in a white nurse's uniform walked up to the big man and said softly, *"If you refuse to eat your peas, I won't let you watch the football game. Open up big."* Creed glared at her in a mixture of anger—at the intrusion—and stark puzzlement—she must have just escaped from the nut house. The teenager was too drunk to notice. She continued as if the nurse had never been there.

"Not from you, I won't. If you did manage to get it in, it'd be too small to feel." The girls broke out in inebriated giggles. "I heard all fat men have little pricks." More giggling.

"You got a real dirty mouth, chicky."

"Well, it's for sure you couldn't fill it." Again, giggles.

Jesus, are all the young ones little bitches like this? Drunk or not, there's no excuse for a filthy mind like that. What are these kids coming to. Probably on dope, too . . .

. . . And the goddamn cop refuses to give them a sobriety test. It took the cocksucker forty-five minutes to get here, so probably they'd have passed it

anyway. Jesus! The truck's going to be in the shop for a week . . .

When Creed got mad, his rage wasn't like that of other people. Their anger would usually dissipate in a few minutes, hours, days. Creed held a stainless steel grudge—forever.

In high school, back in Texas, there had been a bully who'd learned that the hard way. Some scenes from junior high and high school had been triggered, and the memories had fed off each other while they were waiting for the police to arrive. The scenes had climaxed in the complete rerun of the wonderful night Wesley Powers had learned how to fly.

As long as he could remember, Creed had been big for his age—soft, always the brunt of the fat-boy jokes. "Hey, fat Ronnie, broke any seats lately?"

In eighth grade, a desk had broken when he'd sat down in it for English class. Creed suspected someone had tampered with it. In eighth grade he already weighed two-twenty. The football coaches had been after him to play ball for them the next year, but he didn't have any interest. The only interests he had were guns, spending time in the woods with his grandfather, and making music.

By the time he'd reached high school, he'd learned to play all the brass instruments, violin, cello and string bass, drums, and, especially, piano, which was helped along by private lessons every Wednesday from a teacher in town. There was band, orchestra, and chorus. After school it was dance band. The band director played club dates seven nights a week and always encouraged the kids to jam. He also taught them theory and music history.

In his sophomore year, a junior by the name of Wes Powers had taken it upon himself to make Creed his special project. Because Creed was big, and not athletic—a wimp musician—he was a perfect target.

"Hey, lardass, blow any horn-y dicks lately?

"Hey, Creed, how's your skin flute doin'? Care to blow my giant tuba?

"Hey, faggot, get your pussy out of my way. You're giving me a hard-on."

Creed put up with it for months. Powers, who was usually surrounded by his minions, liked to wait outside the cafeteria after lunch. Then he'd follow the big kid all the way to class, taunting, jeering, playing to his cronies.

One day while Creed was eating, the bastard had walked up to the table with a tray of double-serving spaghetti. "Hiya, lardass. Hungry?" There was the trick Marx Brothers trip, and the fat boy ended up wearing the meal.

Creed finally decided the time had come when his unwanted friend embarrassed him in front of Becky.

Powers and his friends had pantsed Creed two or three times. It took six of them to do it, and it was usually when not too many people were around—on the empty baseball field or in the locker room hall of the football stadium after a pep band rehearsal. The degradation was limited to the immediate area, and although it made Creed furious, it wasn't bad enough—yet.

The straw that broke ... had been a girl. Creed had a crush on a cheerleader named Becky Thayer. He liked to fantasize himself as Tom Sawyer and Becky as Becky Thatcher. He knew he'd never get a date with her. She was pretty, had legs like Raquel Welch, was popular, effervescent—everything a six-foot-one fat boy with zits could dream of and never have.

His gym class was the same period as Becky's. It was one of his greatest joys—spotting her and keeping her in view in her gym shorts, blond hair bouncing.

It was a cold, rainy day, and both boys' and girls' classes were in the gym. Before they departed for the teachers' lounge, and cigarettes, the gym teachers had not bothered to pull the huge folding doors across the floor and divide the gym in half. The boys were playing basketball; the girls were playing volley-ball.

Powers must have been walking by the open door to the hall. He'd bided his time, and when Creed's back was turned, amidst the gym's multi-echoed shrieks and thumps, he'd somehow got behind the fat boy, signaled his intentions to everybody in the gymnasium, and yanked Creed's XL gym shorts and jock all the way to the floor. The fat boy also happened to be a skin in the basketball game, something he always hated, so the two classes were treated to everything there was to know about Ronnie Creed.

The gym fell immediately silent, and in the pregnant second, and three-fourths, it took the panicked fat boy to squat and grab his pants, things actually got worse! Creed had eaten three plates of beans and franks for lunch, and the elephantine fart he'd been holding broke loose. The silence exploded in bleacher-shaking flatulence.

Baarrrraaaakkkk! Fraackkk! Pecck!

It escaped in three pieces.

Pandemonium struck like a tsunami.

Creed lumbered for the locker room door leaving sixty kids in helpless, debilitating laughter. Many were literally rolling on the floor, too weak to stand. His last glimpse of the gym centered Becky Thayer bracing her back against the wall, holding her sides, with tears and mascara rolling down her cheeks.

By the seventh period, there wasn't a person in school who didn't know what had happened to Ronnie Creed. For the remainder of the year, "lard-ass" became "fartass." For a sophomore sociopath, it was devastating.

Three months later, Creed got his chance. It was another one of those little delicacies that fate wafts at one's nose.

The flat, West Texas town's water tower stood on a twenty-foot cliff that overlooked one end of a small reservoir. It was a favorite hangout for the kids who wanted to smoke dope, drink, shoot the bull, or add the current graffito to the years of accumulation gone before. The public works department had long ago given up painting out the class graduation years and their slogans, or "Bobby Lee X Shirley forever."

A jogging track ran between the tower and the edge of the cliff, and the village had built a pipe railing at the cliff's edge to keep anyone from falling into the mucky shallows below.

Sixteen-year-old Ronnie Creed was walking home from a firemen's band rehearsal. There was an expectant thunderstorm that had been building ever since the sun had blowtorched its way into the horizon about half an hour before—it was almost dark. Part of Creed's path home followed the jogging path beneath the water tower. He spotted Powers, alone, sitting on the lower pipe of the two-pipe railing with his arms draped over the top. He was facing toward the reservoir, cigarette in one hand, a can of Lone Star in the other.

The fat boy put his horn case down and scoured the surrounding acres for any observers. There were none. Then he looked for a weapon. There it was—a four-foot piece of rusty pipe left over from the railing. It was half buried in the red soil. It came free from the earth just about thirty seconds before Bob Matthews turned on the police cruiser's siren to pull over an out-of-town speeder. The siren covered any sound of Creed's advance until the last split second. He swung the pipe with both hands and all his strength, and sensing imminent danger, Powers turned. It caught him in the side of the face and literally splattered him all over the railing and the path.

The storm hit with a fury, but it did nothing to deter Creed's fifteen minute climb to the top of the tower. He carried Powers's body in a fireman's carry. It was dangerous and exhausting, but the fat body was a lot stronger than it looked, and there was all that adrenaline. Besides, no one would be out here to catch him in the middle of a thunderstorm. And if lightning hit the tower, he wouldn't have to worry about it any more anyway.

He dumped the body on the circular walkway and sat down with his back against the tank to rest. The rain battered the tower with a sustained metallic pinging, but the soaking didn't bother him. Nothing could have bothered him at that point. The replay of Power's head disintegrating gave him an incredible high.

When he finally caught his breath, he rolled the body over the side and was unable to hold back the whoop of delight when the head caught the pipe railing on the ground. The corpse dropped outside the fence, bounced on the cliff's rim, and limply slid over the edge to splat into the reservoir's mud and weeds below. It was not the first time Creed had taken a life, but it certainly was the best.

The body wasn't discovered until the next afternoon. They ruled the death an accidental fall; said the idiot was probably drunk and had climbed the tower before the storm. He had either slipped or a lightning strike had knocked him off.

Six days after the girl had hit his pickup, there was still a clear picture in his mind of Becky Thayer holding her sides in helpless laughter. He could still remember every detail of that day. The little bitch who had run into his truck was just like her. She even looked like her. And, to top it off, they were both named Becky.

Once more fate had intervened in Creed's life.

"It must be a sign from God." He laughed to himself. Sessions had slowed down, and Creed had spent the better part of five days sitting and cruising the block in different Rent-a-Wrecks to establish any routine she had. Never two consecutive days, never the same car twice—always changing clothes two or three times a day—fake mustache, beard; different hats, sunglasses—never letting anyone see that the same man had spent so much time in the neighborhood.

One night he had even sneaked down the back alley that bisected the block and popped all the alley lights with a pellet gun. He'd been able to get close to the house, found her room.

Her routine had given him the plan. It was summer vacation for the kids, and on the weeknights, she was baby-sitting at a house six doors down the street. She walked home a little after eleven o'clock each night when the kid's mother came home from work.

At eleven o'clock, he popped the two necessary streetlights with the pellet gun and parked the truck halfway between the houses. At eleven-oh-five he got out of the truck with his "field kit." The sidewalk was lined with huge elm trees, and he melted into one in his camo outfit, careful not to move in case someone just happened to be looking out a window in the right direction.

At ten after eleven he spotted her coming out the door and down the steps. Hiding from her sight behind one of the trees, he waited to soak the dish towel with ether until she was about forty feet from him on the sidewalk. He knew he was downwind, so she wouldn't catch a hint of the smell.

She never knew what hit her . . .

. . . Until she woke up tied to the tree next to the quicksand swamp where Tommy Dishane and his 240 Z were stewing. Creed had tied her with her back to the tree, hands and legs spreadeagled. There were several slabs of adhesive tape over her mouth. He'd left her clothes on. The snapped ammonia capsule brought her around quickly. Panic was immediate in her eyes as Creed hit them with the flashlight beam.

"Well, dirty mouth, we meet again."

He was answered with unintelligible screams blocked by the tape. And tears.

"My, my, my. And you said my dick wasn't big enough for you. Well you were right, missy. All your holes are just too stretched—I wouldn't be able to feel a thing."

More muffled screams. She was tied much too tightly to squirm.

"And that's exactly why I brought my trusty Ronco Custom Cuntmaker."

He shined the light on the Black & Decker rechargeable electric drill with a one-and-one-half-inch wood bit.

"Friends, with your very own Ronco Custom Cuntmaker, you too can move your honey's pussy to any spot that is convenient. Just send us nineteen-ninety-eight, plus six-ninety-five postage and handling . . ."

There were a lot more muffled screams and tears.

"And now, we'd like to give you a free demonstration. First of all, you must prepare your area."

The razor-sharp survival knife appeared in the light, and he slowly and deliberately cut off her clothing.

"Well, not much to look at." He fondled an underdeveloped breast with his hand and panned the light over a downy crotch. "But with a few improvements, I'm sure we can fix it to feel better than it looks." The big man was getting a hard-on. As he removed his camo jeans it sprang to attention. He wasn't wearing underwear.

"My, my, my. Look at that, will you!" He shined the light on his erection. There were renewed muffled screams.

He walked up to her and touched her belly with the glans. Now this is where that cute little twat should really be. As you can see, it's much too low where it is now. He switched on the drill and began making the new hole.

Had her mouth not been taped, her subsequent screams, when he entered her, would have depilated the bark on all the trees within a hundred feet.

"Will you look at that? You've made another mess down there. Shame, shame! . . . Well, let's get you cleaned up."

CHAPTER ELEVEN

I

Sanger had the new sectioned anus spread out in a porcelain pan. The box had turned up at the Nollensville Road Station.

"I know it's a woman, but I can't be absolutely sure of the age, Joe. I would say young. Could be your missing sixteen-year-old. One thing's for sure."

"What's that?"

"We finally got a real dis-assed-*her* on our hands." The black pupil looked over the top of the crooked dissection glasses for the reaction. Getting none, as usual, he continued, "We'll do skin and blood analyses and a DNA fingerprint for future references—in case there's a body found that might be missing something."

"Dead or alive?"

"Dead first. Scared. Very scared."

"Shit."

"No. Feces. Lots—you can see—covered."

"Shit. Too young. Too damn young."

Farley was convinced the anus belonged to the

sixteen-year-old girl who had disappeared the night before. It was a strong gut feeling, and the guts were rarely wrong.

Missing Persons wouldn't take a report for forty-eight hours, but in this case, it looked like kidnapping. Her keys had been found in the grass next to the sidewalk, three doors from her house. It had to have been well planned—late at night. The two streetlights in the immediate vicinity appeared to have been shot out.

The killer must have stalked her house, too—three more lights had been shot out along the back alley. There was a hole in each globe. An internal alarm had sounded when Farley had stepped on broken glass for the second time. Neighbors verified that the lights on the street had been working earlier in the evening.

Somebody had deliberately taken the time to learn her schedule—knew she was baby-sitting and would come home late. Who the hell would bother taking the time to learn the schedule of a sixteen-year-old kid? A jilted boyfriend? A jealous girlfriend? No. Kids didn't go that far. Even if one of her enemies was mad enough, or psychotic enough to kill her, kids didn't have the right stuff to do that kind of horrible cutting. Besides, all the previous little gifts left for the Police Department had belonged to men.

"No, I'd say this guy has, or had, a grudge to settle, Inspector—because of the dissection bit."

"What makes you so sure, Doc?"

Farley was on his third visit to Samuel Holbrook, this time in the doctor's private practice office in Green Hills. Mornings the psychiatrist taught at Vanderbilt Medical School. Afternoons and evenings he played Sigmund Freud.

"Oh, I'm not sure. But you don't go through the difficulty of cutting out something as repulsive as a rectum for the fun of it. It's a signification. He's telling us in no uncertain terms that these people were assholes and deserved to die."

"But the switch from men to a young girl?"

The pathology report had come back midmorning. It was a young girl—probably middle teens. A dermatologist had confirmed the elasticity constituent and desquamation rate of the skin. A laser spectrograth had established that there were both bath oils and baby powder on the skin's surface—not the kind of pampering to be found on a man.

"It's possible he got temporarily sidetracked. Maybe she did something he didn't like and interrupted his pattern."

"If the rectums we've received belong to the missing musicians, the pattern is shot to hell."

"Well, maybe not a pattern in the sense of a planned sequence, although we can't rule that out. Most psychotics kill when an urge overwhelms them. The desire may be triggered by anything—traveling a certain highway at a certain time of the year; it could be a combination of colors and patterns—say black and yellow checks; a musical work—the second

135

movement of Beethoven's Fifth; the face-reddening embarrassment inflicted by a peer. All kinds of things can trigger the urge. After it's set off, then he may select a victim, God only knows for what reason. And then sometimes if someone just rubs them the wrong way, they go bonkers. The most remarkable thing is they are not guided by ingrained rules and regulations like you and me—a conscience. They have no remorse for the things they've one, and they have no sense, or fear, of consequences. Their aberrant behavior is of no significance to them. It's not a matter of right and wrong; it's a matter of knowing what they can get caught for. There's nothing wrong with taking a life; it's just a nuisance to have to avoid getting caught."

"That's interesting."

"In Vietnam I treated a soldier who had killed fifteen of his own buddies over a period of six months—mostly officers. He admitted this to me. Eight of them he shot in the back in the middle of firefights. The others he murdered on base and buried the bodies. Hated authority. It was only by chance that they even caught him. A wounded man, one the killer thought was dead, happened to see him deliberately shoot a lieutenant in the back of the head during a firefight. The wounded man recovered and turned the killer in. The man was a true sociopath and had no remorse whatsoever over killing his buddies. An interesting sidelight—when they took him to jail, he had to leave his pet dog. He cried like a baby for days."

"Amazing."

"Most sociopaths are extremely cunning—above-average intelligence. And they will go to elaborate lengths to avoid capture. This case is different because he's sending you the evidence of what he's done."

"Brave. Why?"

"He's saying the world is powerless to catch him." The doctor shifted his weight in the huge chair and went on. "And furthermore, what makes the sociopathic personality so difficult to deal with, is the fact that none of the above have to be true."

"Marvelous."

"The only real rule is there don't have to be any rules."

II

Creed was losing weight. He'd noticed for a month now his clothes were getting larger on him. He even went shopping and bought a couple pairs of new jeans. He hadn't weighed himself in fifteen years. Weighing had always depressed him.

He felt so good about the weight loss, he joined a health club and started daily workouts. He'd never had this privilege. His whole life he'd had the urge to eat. Many nights he'd get out of bed for the sole reason of raiding the refrigerator. Quality food was not necessary. He could be just as satisfied with three bags of potato chips as he could with a five-course dinner. One time in college, he had eaten twenty-one hot dogs at one sitting. Another time, he'd eaten three dozen hard-boiled eggs. It was extremely pleasurable. It was also unfortunate that it made your belly lop over your belt.

"Ron, why don't you go to a diet clinic. Lose some serious weight. Man, you've got the frame to house a super body. You've just been hiding it all these years."

So he joined a weight-loss clinic. They gave him special food for all three meals a day. They also demanded he come to group therapy sessions, but he always managed to find an excuse. "Sorry, had to work again."

In three weeks, he'd dropped another twenty pounds. All told, he estimated he'd lost almost forty pounds. His weight on the clinic's scales was two hundred ten. It was the least he'd weighed since junior high, and he felt great.

On top of the health club weight work, he started jogging. At first he could only run a few hundred feet without slowing to a walk. But he kept at it, and the result was dramatic. When he got so he could run a whole mile without stopping, another switch kicked in. It was like eating potato chips—he couldn't do just one mile. Within four weeks he was running four miles a day. The weight continued to fall off. Muscles sprouted in place of fat, and he was constantly bombarded with compliments and questions.

"Hey, Ron. What'd you do, fall in love?"

"Ronnie, look at the size of you. What are you doing to yourself—look's great."

"Hey, Creed, you're going to waste away to nothing."

The compliments were nice, but they had nothing to do with his staying on the weight program, running, and continuing with the clinic. He finally quit when he got down to one-ninety. There wasn't any fat left, and the habits had sunk in. Who was it that said if you do something every day for three weeks, you will have spawned a habit?

No more did he raid the refrigerator in the middle of the night or between meals. He liked the way he looked in the mirror. Without the fat, his face had turned rather handsome.

He grew a beard. It was a lighter shade than the long, dark-brown hair on his head.

For the first time, he noticed that the green eyes were a complement to the rest of his face. Grandfather's Indian blood was supposed to give rise to dark eyes. Creed was proud of his Indian blood and had always been a little ashamed of the incongruity.

With his face thinned down, the slightly hawk-billed nose he'd always been self-conscious about seemed to fit nicely.

He decided to change his hair, and for the first time in his life, he went to a fancy hairstyling salon.

He told the lady to cut it off—to give him a styling. When he'd returned home, he'd been pleasantly surprised when the unfamiliar handsome face had stared back at him for half an hour in the bathroom mirror. He preened this way and that, finally succumbing to stripping off his clothes and mugging naked in front of the bedroom's full-length mirror for another half hour.

With the increased approval in his physical looks came an increased desire to get rid of the idiots who were holding him back from the successful career and the kind of recognition he deserved. It was time he bore down and exercised his God-given right. He would be careful, but the competition was about to thin.

III

In the first two weeks of September, three more musicians, the owner of a truck body shop, an IRS auditor, and a State Farm agent disappeared. A total of six boxes labeled "POLICE" turned up in four main-branch police stations. Two of them appeared in one day.

Farley was afraid he was going to have a heart attack before they got a line on what the hell was happening to the music community. When he was in the office, the phone rang constantly with calls from the

American Federation of Musicians, the American Federation of Television and Radio Artists, the Screen Actors Guild, and a number of part-time musicians who didn't belong to any union at all. The department had not been successful in suppressing the story after six "pickers" disappeared in two weeks. In addition to two male singers, two arrangers, another producer, and a keyboard player turned up missing.

There was a cry of outrage that hit the national news programs and the wire services around the world.

NASHVILLE MUSICIANS DISAPPEARING

MURDER, MUTILATION SUSPECTED

It wasn't easy, but the reporters mangaged to let the public know that the police had received over one dozen mutilated anuses in the last three months. The asshole jokes that were flying around news rooms worldwide could have filled a small book.

IV

The IRS auditor had been the most satisfying. Creed had waited six months to get him.

The spring before, Creed had got the notification to come to the Federal Building for a routine audit. Because he'd always done his own taxes, he'd have to stand it without the backup help of a professional CPA. Creed had always been one of the suckers who never kept receipts or wrote everything down. It was in his head.

Sensing blood, the auditor tore him to pieces, throwing out deduction after deduction, smugly punching the adding machine over and over. It wasn't the money that bothered the big man, it was losing to a shark who was enjoying systematically shortening the arms and legs of a swimmer boxed in a barrel. The frenzy had gone on for an hour, and finally, for the first time in his life, Creed lost his cool. It came in two stages:

The first stage was over a deduction on a three thousand dollar Revox two-track tape recorder he'd bought. He'd got it for a song from another musician who had come on hard times and was moving back home to Iowa. Creed had failed to get a receipt and had no idea where the guy would be today, four years later.

"Oh, you don't have the receipt? I'm sorry, but I can't allow the deduction. If you find it, please bring it in and we'll adjust your credit."

"But you can come to the house and look at the damn machine."

The auditor had been polite, but always firm with a smile.

"I'm sorry, Mr. Creed. We've got to have documentation as to where and when you bought it." He

142

clicked off another fifteen hundred dollars of tax credit.

"You're gonna buy it, cocksucker."

"Now, Mr. Creed, I know you have no intentions of threatening a federal officer. Let's just keep our heads."

Oh, I'll keep mine, but yours is a foregone conclusion, you little fucker.

The second stage came when the auditor threw out the entire year of seventy-five-percent business write-off Creed claimed on the truck. Most studio musicians were allowed to write off their mileage to and from sessions because their offices were in their own homes.

"Mr. Creed, do you have the daily log of your mileage?"

"No, of course not. I was never told you needed one."

"Without it, I cannot accept this deduction."

If the auditor had been in a better mood that day, he might have given Creed a chance to try to construct one, but the greasy little man had just found out the night before that his eighteen-year-old daughter was having an affair with one of the deacons at his church who was twice her age. Nothing was going to stand in the way of his revenge on the world. From now on the precious American taxpayer was going to know the unforgettable feeling of the RAPE—the Rapid Anal Piston Effect—life's giant green weenie up the bazoo. And he would enjoy every minute of shoving it in and out.

—He would enjoy every minute of it only for another six months.

Creed blew. Red-faced, veins bulging, he stood up and without a word, grabbed the auditor's huge GI metal desk and flipped it over onto the floor—all four hundred pounds. The terrified agent backpedaled in his desk chair just fast enough to escape getting crushed under the monster. The office was a shambles. Papers, government forms A through Z, file covers, desk implements, and an IBM personal computer carpeted the floor.

"Have it your way, twatface," he rasped. "You can send me a bill." The violence in the big man's face froze the auditor's blood in his veins. The agent would not sleep for weeks, swearing that he had seen straight into hell in those eyes.

There should have been a serious prosecution. Federal agents should have broken down his front door and sent him to Leavenworth. But after a week, the big man stopped wondering if they were going to appear. Evidently, the touchhole had chickened out. Creed had hoped an undertoned sentiment of certain revenge had been conveyed.

In the meantime, he found out where the auditor lived and got a handle on his schedule. He'd checked periodically since then to make sure the little bastard would be available when he wanted him. The guy's routine didn't vary a minute week after week.

Creed let the six months go by so that his name wouldn't be in front of the police when they investigated who the cocksucker had been auditing. Six months was enough. The grudge had not diminished one iota, and in the rampage Creed went on to celebrate his new looks and body, he figured he could squeeze the little prick into his schedule.

Tied around a tree on the banks of Kentucky Lake, little by little the screaming auditor lost his head, his skin—foot by square foot, and his anus—and not necessarily in that order. Another body was relegated to Davey Jones's auxiliary locker.

CHAPTER TWELVE

I

The police chief had allotted fifteen men to the mutilations. In some quiet, closed, police circles, it had been nicknamed the "disaster caper"—but only after the female anus had turned up.

Newspaper descriptions of what the police were receiving were couched in careful, anatomically correct terminology. It made for boring reading, but the papers' circulation improved by almost twenty percent.

Television wasn't so easy. Good taste had balked at the words "anus" or "rectum" being verbalized in bulk quantities. Most reporters just referred to the fact that the victim had been brutally mutilated. However, one reporter from Channel 6 had actually had the guts to use, "Mulilated posterior body part." In newsrooms around the city the man had been toasted, and thereafter unaired terminology had taken on a government anagram—MPBP—pronounced meepbeep. When the news of another murder, any murder, came into any news office, the first question was, "Did the victim have a missing meepbeep?"

Joe Farley was put in charge of the police task force, but the investigators remained frustrated and powerless because of the lack of bodies.

Farley had not been sleeping well. He was constantly fighting one bug, or another. He'd had the same cold twice. Not even Nero Wolfe could come up with a solution when there were not enough pieces to afford deductions.

The gray-haired detective stood in front of the fifteen men in the squad room of Downtown Metro. He wished there was a podium. His five-nine height always gave him an inferiority complex when standing before a crowd of men. He wished he were six-two or had the guts to wear lifts. And there was the constant bulge battle that he was now beginning to lose, which made him look even shorter. Whenever someone kidded him about his new potbelly, his standard reply was, "I'm pregnant. Gonna be an elephant. Trunk's already hanging out."

Farley looked up from the papers on the lectern in front of him and said, "Okay, Brauer, Cowens, Delaney—you take the first three victims on the missing list. They're all musicians. We've broken the list up into musicians and all others. We want names of their relatives, friends, dogs, cats, and pet mice— and, for damn sure, the pet nicknames of their Wednesday-afternoon mistresses. No stone is too small to be left unturned."

He was holding a list of some forty-five missing persons. Probably not all of them, indeed, if any of them, were buried somewhere without their rectums intact. The problem was, there was no way of knowing without going through the whole list.

"Lyles, Monroe, Openheim—the next three are yours."

He paused to look up at the men to explain, "Most of you know by now that we're going to feed it all into Hewey and see what he regurgitates." Hewey was the Hewlett Packard mainframe that had cost the taxpayer almost two million dollars. It was hooked into a nationwide crime network. "If there's a common name to all these people, we'll have a good idea who's got the knife and the strong smell about him."

He finished the assignments and dismissed the men. It would probably take a week to collect the data.

The next day there were two more missing persons reports—an air force recruiter and another bass singer.

II

Creed did not have to work. Even when he was in elementary school he'd known his grandfather had been old-Texas money—unusual for a half-breed Indian. The boy had never known how much money until after the old man had died and left it all to his daughter. Uranium, she had told her son. Grandfather had made a fortune in uranium, then oil.

She had invested and lived off the interest, sending the Creed to college, buying his first car—a new MG convertible when he was only eighteen. They'd always lived in a comfortable house, and growing up, Creed pretty much had everything he wanted, including a dozen musical instruments.

The only thing he'd grown up without had been a father. His father had had the lack of foresight to have a heart attack when Creed was only three. He could still remember the chaos on the night the rescue squad and three police cars answered the emergency call. His father had been dead by the time they got him to the hospital.

The wealthy old half-breed took over raising the boy. By the time Creed was five, the two of them had made wilderness trips throughout the southwest mountains and high plains. The gray-haired, pigtailed *cherchinka* had known the area intimately and had taught the youngster things most hard-core survivalists would never learn. He was the only person Creed had come close to loving; he was the only person who knew Creed was not like normal kids, and he'd chosen to take that secret with him to the grave. He had died the day Creed entered his junior year in high school.

Through the years, his mother had carefully nurtured her only child's unusual musical abilities—getting him the right piano teachers, the advanced theory tutoring from a retired music professor, even renting, then buying the musical instruments he wanted. But she'd done it from a distance. There was always a great void between them. She never showed any physical affection——no hugs and kisses——and that was fine with him. He didn't need it or want it. Grandfather was sufficient. After he was gone, Creed found he didn't need anyone.

On his twenty-first birthday, his mother had told him that she had set up a trust fund to help him establish a career. It was as if she were divorcing herself from ever having anything to do with her strange son again. Creed was dumbfounded when she'd told him it was five million dollars.

"Mother, can we afford that much?"

"Ronnie, your grandfather left you and me a little over forty million dollars. Even after our expenses, the principle still increases each year. If anything ever happens to me, you get it all. You know that there are no other relatives in this family. Grandfather was the last of the line. It's up to you."

Creed couldn't believe they were that wealthy. She had always been careful with money. Through the years to come, he would find that he had inherited her talent to handle it. The bottom line was he did not have to work. The music was a love, a passion. He could get high on something as simple as a Chopin prelude and easily lose an evening playing Bach or Brahms on the forty-thousand-dollar Steinway grand his mother had bought him when he'd graduated from North Texas summa cum laude.

He also got high on death—any death—beast, bird, fish, or human. His mother had given up buying pets by the time he was five. They just never seemed to live very long.

"What happened to your hamster, Ronnie?"

"Don't know, Mom. It just died."

The overweight fat kid savored death like a gourmet savors food. By junior high, the local funeral home had had to run him off the premises more than once.

A month after he'd graduated from college, he'd gone to a Barbara Mandrell concert with a drummer friend who knew one of Barbara's guitar players. Talking to the guitarist backstage after the concert, the man mentioned that their keyboard player was leaving the following week. Creed asked how he could go about auditioning for the job. Mandrell was cool. He knew that she performed a wide range of music in addition to the country tunes. Besides, Creed had listened to country music since he was old enough to turn on the radio. In high school he'd played bass in a country band for three years.

He got the job.

For the first time, he was a full-time professional, and he loved it. However, he discovered that he was overqualified for the job. Doing the same concert night after night got to be a bore. About the only playing the band did was rehearsing the tunes for the show or the actual performance. There wasn't any time to play anything else. They were either traveling, rehearsing, setting up, or tearing down.

Uncle Sam rescued him, and the twenty-two-year-old didn't have a choice.

Creed was one of the last men in the United States to get drafted before the draft was done away with. Rather than get shot at, he enlisted in the air force band program.

Except for the fact that it was the military, replete with all its bullshit, the first two years weren't bad. He played piano in the seventeen-piece big band that played officer and NCO clubs, in addition to bigwig government parties. Rarely did a week go by that he failed to augment the book by at least one new arrangement.

In addition, there was the fifty-piece concert band in which he played percussion.

His second year in the band, he started a hot Four Freshman–style quartet backed by their own instruments.

The third year, the band got a new commander—a musically lopsided prick who was a stickler for air force spit and polish. His idea of a good time was a concert comprised entirely of marches. The first thing the new commander did was eliminate the quartet. Five of the band's best musicians quickly retired, and ten more lifers requested, and were granted, transfers to other bands.

The prick cut down the dance band to start a couple of his own pet projects—a German oom-pa-pa band and a bagpipe corps.

By the end of five months, there were a number of men who hated the commander enough to kill him if they thought they could have got away with it.

Creed did it—and got away with it.

"Hey, Joe. Somebody from Kroger on line six."

"Thanks."

Farley walked from the file cabinet to the phone and stabbed the flashing light that was one of the four homicide buttons.

"This is Farley."

"Yes, sir. This is John Hatchey. I'm the butcher at the Dickerson Road Kroger."

"Yes." Farley had an uneasy feeling for what he thought was coming.

"Sir, I think you better get over here. We found something in the display case that ain't ours. We didn't put it there."

"Is it what I'm afraid it is?"

"I think it is. It's hard to tell."

Farley hung up the phone and hollered at Buck Lee McClulland, who was three desks away poking at an old Adler electric typewriter. McClulland had been assisting Farley with some of the paperwork, and Farley had decided he just didn't want to face this one alone.

"Hey, Buck Lee."

"Yut."

"Wanna go for a ride?"

"What's cookin'?"

"Probably some sautéed rectum. It's on sale in the Kroger meat section today."

"Oh, God. I'll say one thing for this psycho—he's got a helluva sense of humor."

The anus was neatly packaged in a Styrofoam tray that was wrapped in cellophane. There was a faded "ground round" store label on it that had been written over with a Magic Marker. It said "prime asshole."

The skin on the meat looked like it had belonged to a black person. It had been washed clean and lacked the Ivory Snow coloring that had been characteristic of all the others after they had been cleaned. There was a keyboard player reported missing who was black. He had been a very small man—about five feet. His nickname had been Ballsy—partly from a corruption of his name, Hawlsey, and partly because he was an extremely good player, having at one time toured with Aretha Franklin.

When they got into the car, Farley said to McClulland, "Let's take this to Sanger and see if he can determine the size of the man from the size of our little gift here."

"I'm game."

Sanger took one look at it and said, "Is he doing kids now? That's a kid's, Farley." He turned it around and studied it some more. "Wait ... No ... Too much hair. Let me put a hair under the stereo."

"I think it's the little keyboard player that's missing."

Sanger scraped a hair off the piece of meat with a scalpel and put it under the microscope. After adjusting it for a few seconds he turned around and said, "You're right. It's an adult black. Sure was a small one, though. Looks like a kid."

Farley turned to McClulland and said, "Goddamn this son of a bitch. What's he doing with the bodies?"

At that very moment, two giant slabs of rock on either side of one of Tennessee's numerous faults slipped, causing an earthquake too small to be detected by anything other than machines. It was just enough to cause gasses at the bottom of Creed's favorite quicksand swamp to flatulate four of the eight bodies to the surface. Two of them broke the surface in still-frame action and in plain view of a bow hunter in a tree stand a few yards from Creed's favorite whipping-post oak tree. The man almost fell out of the tree when he put the binoculars on the swamp's small disturbance and saw a horrified, but for sure dead, pale and horribly bloated face staring back at him.

Farley finally got his bodies to play with. Heavy equipment dredged up four more and a Datsun 240 Z.

But even after all the bodies had been autopsied and the tortures they had endured had been revealed, the closest the detective would come to catching the killer would be when Creed's name appeared on the computer list of coincidental acquaintances of the Missing Persons victims.

It was two weeks later that Officer Aaron Delaney showed up at the big man's doorstep for the sixth time after finding no one home for the first five. Creed opened the door with a pleasant grin and said, "Yes, sir, what can I do to you this fine autumn evening."

CHAPTER THIRTEEN

I

He'd been roller-skating, holding hands with one of the junior high cheerleaders, when he felt the entry. The sudden combination of pain and ecstasy in such a sensitive part of the body had caused him to stagger and fall. He knew she was with one of the high school football players, knew she was in the backseat of the boy's old Pontiac in an unlit section of the church parking lot. The jock was not all that big—five-eleven, one seventy-five, but his swollen organ was huge. Funny, in the showers the guy wasn't any larger than anybody else. She was in a state of delirious pain/joy. The pumping became faster, faster, and he bolted from the rink area into the men's room and slammed the stall door closed. When she finally climaxed, he screamed with her. He had only just got his pants down in time.

II

The two things Jerry was dreading the most turned out to be pleasant surprises.

First, the IRS audit was a breeze. It had taken place in his CPA's office, and the man who was doing the auditing was attentive, polite, and seemed genuinely interested in his client as a person. Jerry'd had the fantasy of being torn to financial pieces by a vicious little megalomaniacal bureaucrat who was intent on making his job-justifiable quota or points for a promotion.

The musician had always kept meticulous records—right down to documenting the purchase of every last postage stamp. Everything was scrupulously categorized and totaled. The auditor had suggested a deduction neither Jerry nor the CPA had realized was available, and the end result was that the musician would actually get a refund of almost three hundred dollars.

On the same day, when he returned to the house, a check for the total amount of his wrecked Saab was waiting for him in the mail. He deposited it and went car shopping. The insurance company had paid for a brand-new car when a young girl on medication had gone to sleep, accelerated to over fifty, according to witnesses, and creamed the four-month-old Saab while it was parked in front of the dry cleaners. It was a good thing Jerry hadn't been in it.

For having to do no more than show up at the IRS office, the day had turned a new car and three hundred dollars. By seven o'clock that night, the paperwork was finished on the new Saab Turbo 900. He hadn't been able to get a white one. The only one equipped the way he wanted was black, and Jerry had never been excited over a black car. In the summer, you could literally fry an egg on it from the sun's absorbed heat. "We'll order a white one, Mr. Cayce, but they're running three to five months on delivery. If you're lucky, it'll be here for Christmas." Black was also harder to keep clean. However, a black car was better than no car. Driving home, he silently cursed the girl who had totaled his white one.

He still had mixed feelings after he'd put the new car in the garage and come in the kitchen door. Lauren's car wasn't in its usual spot, and he decided he'd surprise her with his windfall when she got home. She wouldn't see it in the garage; she always parked under the carport and came in the side door.

When he'd left the house that morning, he'd been cursing Meluttle Sebastion Young, Internal Revenue Service, like a sailor with a stubbed toe. A card had been sent with the audit notification, and with a name like that, this guy had to be a dick with four balls.

"That bastard is going after my nuts with a vise grip, Lauren. You know they never call you in unless they've got something on you."

"Jerry, that's simply not true. The computer probably kicked you out at random. He even told you on the phone that it was only routine." Jerry had had to call and change the first appointment because he'd had sessions.

"Bullshit. He's playing me for a sucker. He'll piss up my nose once he gets me down there. He's going to slice and fry serious ass here, and we both know it." He was pacing up and down the length of the kitchen biting his nails.

"You're worrying about nothing," she'd said confidently.

There was a note on the table saying she'd be late. Lauren's clientele was scattered between several hospitals, nursing homes, and private sanatoriums. One of her patients was dying at Parkside Hospital, and the family had requested her presence. Would he please pick up Ginger from the baby-sitters.

He made the ten-minute drive to pick up Ginger, and they had a tickle fight in the front seat on the way home. Ginger exploited Jerry's incredible ticklishness with great regularity—sometimes at the most inopportune times. With the help of her mother, she had made him pee his pants one time. She'd never quit trying to get a replay.

They stopped by McDonald's to get her a *Happy*

Meal, and Jerry decided he'd wait till he got home to eat. Once Ginger had settled down in her room with her supper and Andy Griffith, Jerry made himself two sandwiches—one banana and peanut butter, and one of eight slices of four different kinds of cold meat, topped with mayonnaise, mustard, and hamburger relish. He grabbed a Coke and a bag of potato chips, and took everything into the den to watch television for a while. Some of the depression had lifted, and his appetite had returned.

After sitting down in the recliner and arranging the food on a tray in his lap, the last thing he remembered was the mind picture of the young girl who wrecked his car—and a local car dealer commercial that sucked a big one. He would remain blacked out until the middle of the night when he was awakened in bed by Lauren's thrashing. She began to grunt loudly while making quick slashing motions with her right arm. Jerry opened his eyes, and was instantly terrified. However, it wasn't from Lauren's dream; it was from the abomination confronting him. Framed in the glow from the yard light, Meluttle Sebastion Young stood at the foot of the bed dripping in blood and gore from head to foot. He was naked and holding his intestines in front of him, piled in both hands. There was a puzzled frown on his face as he looked down at the gore. It was the classic look that said, "This can't be happening to me." He looked up at

Jerry, canted his head in acceptance that it was happening to him, and his face screwed up as he started to cry before Jerry could close his eyes in horror. When he opened them again, the IRS auditor had disappeared.

By breakfast time, the author had almost recovered—at least enough to eat three bagels smothered with cucumber cream cheese. While reading the morning paper, Jerry saw the article on page four about the rape and murder of Marajo Peters. Something clicked in the back of his mind, but it didn't quite register that this was the young girl who had played demolition derby with his Saab. Had he realized this, the listings for the name "Peters" might have jumped out and bitten him when he replaced the telephone book in its usual drawer after someone had left it lying open to page 349 on the kitchen counter.

III

It was Columbus Day.

The plainclothes cop flashed his badge and said, "Mr. Creed, you're a hard man to find. I know it's a holiday, but do you mind if I come in? I have a few questions to ask."

"Certainly, Officer. Come in and have a seat." Creed motioned the man to the long sofa.

"No thanks. This'll only take a minute." He remained by the door.

"Suit yourself. What's this about?"

Ignoring him the cop went on, "You're in the music business, that right?"

"Correct." Creed had seen on the news that the police had found the missing musicians in the quicksand. They would be questioning a lot of musicians. The officer's presence was only a minor irritation. The sooner he was gone, the sooner Creed could go back to the special football game on TV.

"You have a date book, don't you?"

"Certainly."

"Would you mind getting it. I need to know where you were on several different dates."

"Be right back."

The cheers of the Denver fans exploded from the den as the Broncos scored the third unanswered touchdown in a row.

Creed came back into the room with his book.

The cop slowly began to reel off the dates he wanted verified. Creed looked them up one by one. The officer wrote down where the musician had been working on specific dates. It would all go into the computer.

"Did you know any of these people?" The cop showed him a list of about three dozen missing persons."

Creed took the paper and scanned it.

"Yeah, I know Howie Dearsley ... Bugs Bartholomew ... Tim Joince ... Charlie Crouser ... looks like that's it. I don't know these other people."

"When was the last time you saw them? Howie Dearsley ..."

Creed paused to remember for each of them and lied.

"You didn't know any of these others?"

"Not personally. I recognize some of the names, but I've never met them."

"Which ones?"

Creed rattled off seven more names.

"What do you know about them?"

The man was not even asking good questions, and Creed was becoming impatient with his incompetence.

"Officer, what the hell is this? What difference does it make?"

The cop answered with exaggerated patience, "What do you know about them?"

"Jesus, I'm missing the game."

"So am I."

"All right," and Creed went through the other names and designated them as producers, arrangers, or singers.

"Did any of the people you knew ever talk to you about their personal lives?"

"Are you kidding me? How personal? Do they eat their pussy from the top or bottom? Let's see, Howie always eats his wife from the bottom, but his girlfriend from the ..."

"Okay, okay. I asked for that," the cop interrupted. "Let's ..."

Creed interrupted him with, "You're investigating where all the musicians have disappeared to and the murders of the ones found in the swamp. It's all over the news. You want to know who's cutting out assholes, but you're wasting your time here. I didn't do it. I would have nothing to gain doing it, even if I were capable. And anybody who tries to cut my asshole out is going to get his balls stuffed down his throat."

Ignoring him, the detective went on, "What I need to know is if there was any jealousy you knew about in the music circles, somebody with a bad attitude—an "Everybody's an asshole but me" kind of person—any reason you can think of that someone would want to kill and mutilate these men."

"Well, Officer, I'm afraid I'm not much help. I just don't know."

"Mr. Creed, we've analyzed the list of missing and murdered musicians by their instruments or skills." That had been Farley's idea. "We found out something very interesting: Every one of those musicians was either an arranger, a singer, or keyboard player—no guitar players, no drummers. I also happened to notice from the unions' lists that you're in all three of those categories." That had been another one of Farley's ideas.

"So ..."

"How many other musicians in Nashville would you say are specialized in those three areas?"

"Officer, I have no earthly idea. Probably a pile of them. And, incidentally, I also play the strings, bass, all the brass instruments, flute and clarinet, drums and Jew's harp—that help you any?"

"Wouldn't you stand to gain, if part of your competition were removed, Mr. Creed?"

"Buddy, that's uncalled for. So would all the other musicians who do sessions. The difference is, I'm independently wealthy. I don't have to work. If you want to check my bank account, you'll find I wouldn't benefit jack shit from killing those guys."

The detective made more notes, and without looking up, said, "Mr. Creed, you into guns?"

"No. Why?"

"You own a survival knife?"

"No. Why?"

"Where's home originally? You're not from Nashville are you?"

"I'm from West Texas. Small town not far from Pecos."

"What's the name?"

"Storey."

"How do you spell it?"

"Jesus Christ, Officer, look it up. I'm missing the football game for this shit."

The cop was writing in his notebook when he said casually, "*I hope you don't mind if I change the channel to the soaps. Heather is going to tell Bob whether she'll marry him or not."*

Creed looked at the cop as if the man were on fire and vehemently spat, "Fuck off, Cunt!"

Embarrassed for only a second, the officer finished writing, looked up, and said, "Mr. Creed, we can do this downtown, if you'd rather. It doesn't make any difference to me."

Creed answered with a fiery, "Okay, let's go downtown. You drive, bastard!"

Unmollified, the cop continued. "Did you ever see any of these men anywhere besides the studio?"

"Goddamn it, you fucking moron, get the hell out of here! I want to watch the game!"

The cop paused a few seconds as he looked Creed in the eye. Finally he engaged the clutch and opened the door.

"Okay. This'll do for now. I may need to talk to you again."

"Marvelous. Have your girl call mine. Maybe we can do lunch."

The cop put the notebook back into his suit pocket and without looking around, he mumbled, "Good day, Mr. Creed. Have a nice afternoon."

The door closed but Creed had already returned to his den. The game was gone and he was annoyed, but he remained unruffled.

He went back to cleaning the 220 Swift. The .22s were lying on the coffee table along with both silencers. He had gone through five boxes of shells with the Swift, and almost as many with the .22 rifle that afternoon on a three-hundred-acre farm that belonged to a boating acquaintance. Creed had taken the man for rides several times in the jet and had scared the daylights out of him on one occasion when he'd flown the boat across the grass connecting two adjacent islands—at seventy miles an hour.

The football game was becoming an annoyance. Denver had blown the three-touchdown lead, and he turned down the volume with the remote.

After applying a light coat of grease on the guns, he put them away. The Swift and the Browning .22 pistol went back into the gun cabinet; the .22 rifle that had killed Robbie Gilson and the derelict was broken down and placed inside a cotton bag along with both silencers. Then he carried the bag to the pantry, removed the electrical panel, and laid the bundle on a horizontal two-by-four inside the walls.

"I need to find a better place to hide it." He had been going to dig a hole big enough to cover a waterproof box and hide it in a vacant lot across town.

He got another Corona from the refrigerator and went back into the den. He left the TV volume low and eased his large frame into the La-Z-Boy.

Stupid fucking cops. They don't have a thing. Or maybe, Ron, ma boy—maybe, as usual, you're just too smart for the dumb fuckers.

He tipped the chair back to horizontal, and his mind went back to . . .

* * *

". . . the air force. They're just as dumb as the morons in the goddamn air force."

The new commander-director had spent the first weekend inspecting the barracks, the band hall, and even several of the base-housing homes where the married NCOs lived—an unheard of precedent.

He was a major, had been a major longer than any other major in the air force, and was hell-bent on making light colonel. Everything the band did was to make Major Robert J. Fuqua a colonel. He had even taken the band to play a concert for a Brownie Scout den meeting one evening, because the den mother was the wife of the general who would be writing the commander's proficiency report. If there was an officer present who could put in a good word, then Major Fuqua made sure, for one ridiculous reason or another, that the band would serenade him, and replete in its finest spit and polish.

There were frequent inspections that ruined weekend after weekend, and passes were canceled for petty reasons. Article Fifteens, the next step down the ladder from a court-martial, were thrown about like the grass from the lawn mowers manned by lower-ranked airmen who were forced to cut the grounds around the band hall on Saturday mornings. The major said the damned civilians were too lazy to do it right.

All good music ceased and desisted. One by one, the classic band standards were replaced with marches, and whenever new contemporary music came on the market, it was not purchased in order to save money to buy the equipment for the German Guggenheim band or the bagpipe corps.

The majority of the woodwinds and several of the percussionists were ordered to learn the persnickety pipes, and to keep the kilts and accoutrements in spit-shine condition for surprise inspections that could take place even on a Sunday morning.

Creed was forced to learn the bagpipes. He complained bitterly that he was a piano player not a goddamned finger fucker. His protests led to more shit details and some Article Fifteens that cost him two stripes and a month's pay.

The last time Creed had been disciplined, the commander had sent him, for the third time, to the mess hall kitchen on the night detail. The facility was staffed entirely by civilians under contract to the government, and they did not appreciate the military poking its nose in. However, the commander had decided it was a marvelous place to instill discipline— whether the civilians wanted the help or not. The airman was expected to work from midnight till eight A.M., then make the eight-thirty band rehearsal in the morning—clean, and gleaming in spit and polish. He would spend the night cleaning grease off the exhaust hood, scrubbing the huge pots used to cook cereal and soup, scouring the floors in out-of-the-way-hard-to-reach areas, and, in general, any dirty jobs the civilians didn't like to do.

One of the chores the civilians didn't like was loading smelly garbage cans full of meat waste and bones into a van, then driving the stinking van across town to a company that ground up the scraps in large industrial grinders. The pulverized meat and bone was mixed with grain, compressed into pellets, and sold in fifty-pound bags to several industrial catfish farms in the area. The smelly ride was always left for the night shift, and the kitchen had even been entrusted with a key to the company's loading dock door so the cans could be left inside the building and not available to the local animals.

The first time Creed made the meat-wagon run, he had taken a tour of the small factory. It was deserted at two A.M., and the morning shift would not report to work until seven.

The third time he made the run, he was accompanied by a drunken, chloroformed major. Creed had caught him outside the officers' club where he knew the old man spent his evenings religiously, and just as religiously left at one A.M. each morning.

The major awoke abruptly from a broken ammonia capsule. His mouth was taped, he was naked, and he was hanging by tied wrists from the hook of an overhead winch used to lower heavy sides of meat into the huge funnel-top grinder.

The first thing the major saw, when his eyes finally focused, was Creed standing on the platform that surrounded the machine's open top. There was a grin on the big man's face as he showed the major the remote box in his hand.

"Well, Major, fancy meating you in a place like this—that's meat-ing—with an a."

There were the predictable mumbled protests and squirms. They were fruitless. When it finally dawned, through the dangling pain, where he was and what Creed intended, they increased dramatically.

"You're about to make the band and a lot of fish very happy, Commander. That's a remarkable accomplishment for a bonehead like yourself."

"MMMmmmmmm! MMMmmmmmmm!"

"Our only regret—yours and mine—is they'll never know how you gave your life in shameless sacrifice for the good of your country." He stepped back and saluted crisply—"Major Robert J. Fuck-ya made the su-preme sacrifice, his career exemplifying the meritorious conduct becoming to an officer of the U-nited States of 'Merica above and beyond the call of du-tee."

He pressed the button on the remote to start the grinder, and then another button that ordered the winch to slowly lower its burden. He had only turned on minimal light in the factory, and the grinder's whine was not loud enough to be heard outside the building. They had the place all to themselves.

After each six-inch interval, Creed would stop the grinding and raise the officer clear of the machine. The major, face and bloodshot eyes bulging in brilliant red, veins in stark base relief, passed out at one foot, but Creed brought him around with another ammonia capsule.

He was able to keep the maniacally contorting man conscious until the grinding had removed most of his legs. Blood poured from his eyes, nose, and ears from the strain. When the major finally went into deep shock—at the groin—Creed know his playtime was over. He unhooked the body, removed the bindings and tape, then finished the grinding. Boredom was setting in by the time the officer's head had begun to slowly pop and crunch its way through the machine's aperture.

The meat had been deposited in long strings flecked with bone in a large plastic bin on wheels at the bottom of the grinder. The big man pushed the bin to the factory's next stage and dumped its hamburg-like deposit into a vat with several hundred pounds of slow-cooking beef and pork grindings. Then he hosed down the machine and the bin, put the bin back under the grinder, turned out the light, and returned to the kitchen. He was hyped enough not to sleep for the next two nights. The air force never did come up with an explanation for the officer's desertion. With the installment of another commander, the band's routine returned to normal.

CHAPTER FOURTEEN

I

Jerry was once more reclining in the La-Z-Boy, while the TV blathered its usual commercial pabulum geared to the intelligence of a third grader. The pabulum was replaced by *Monday Night Football*, but his mind never saw the kickoff.

The end result of two more mutilations had been manifested—this time at two different grocery chains. One of them belonged to a young girl—and there was a young girl missing—the same one involved in destroying Jerry's Saab. It had taken Lauren to point it out that morning over breakfast. He'd never seen it—had glanced right over it. Had his brain just refused to accept?

"Jerry," she had said, "isn't this the little girl who ran into the Saab?"

"Oh, Sweet Jesus Christ! Please, no."

But it was yes, and it got worse. While they were eating supper and watching the news, Channel 2 had reported that an IRS auditor by the name of Meluttle Sebastion Young had turned up missing. The government feared foul play.

"Foul play," Jerry had thought to himself, "I'd certainly call what happened to that poor man, in the condition I saw him at the foot of my bed, foul play. And what the hell was Lauren doing in her dream?"

Again he had written horrible things in his book, and again, they had come true practically verbatim.

He considered once more just stopping—scrapping the book, but the thought of throwing away hundreds of hours of work went against every fiber in his body.

"Damn it. I'm not doing the killing. I've got alibis—some. Why should I be penalized for this shit. Nobody can say it's my fault he's doing it. Besides, the way New York's been pressuring me to finish? Hell, if I back out on this project now, there won't be a company in the world who'll touch me. 'Bad risk,' they'll say."

After supper, Lauren had gone to visit a patient in a nursing home. As soon as she got home, he was going to have a serious talk with her. She'd wanted him to go see their friend the shrink, and it was time Jerry, The Innocent, got on record. Besides, in his date book, there was a two-week stretch without any sessions. The depression was only magnified by the fact that, apparently, nobody wanted the skills of an almost over-the-hill musician. Gone were the days of arranging for the Johnny Cashes, Kenny Rogerses, Andy Williamses, Dolly Partons, and Barbra Streisands. He had really been something in his heyday.

"I'd kill to arrange an album for Garth Brooks—my name in the credits—country and pop charts. Cat wails when he sings in tune."

II

Sam Bruckstein's office was in a modern medical complex in Green Hills. Although nowhere near the level of old-money Belle Meade or new-money Brentwood, the area was one of Nashville's nicer sections of town. Pricey stores in the resident mall and satellite shopping areas attested to that. Jerry sat in the waiting room even more antsy than usual. His appetite had returned, then left again, and he had dropped another seven pounds. He was almost to the weight he should have been for his size. That was the one redeeming factor of all this—he wasn't disgusted at his naked image in the mirror anymore. He'd always hated his red hair. Compounding that with the fat had made him avoid really looking in mirrors for years. On the way home, maybe he would drop by Dillards and buy a couple pairs of new jeans that fit. If he didn't put the weight back on, he was going to have to buy a whole new wardrobe.

"Dr. Bruckstein is ready for you now, Mr. Cayce."

The receptionist had roused him from his shopping spree. Reluctantly, he followed her into the office where Wild Sam Bruckstein looked up from his desk, saw Jerry, stood up, broke into a massive smile, and came around the desk—all six-feet-six, and one-half, of him—with obvious pleasure at seeing him. Jerry thought to himself that the giant must have gained some more weight. He must top out at close to four hundred pounds.

Wild Sam had got his reputation from several sources. He had been in the news for three decades for one stunt after another. At sixty years of age, he still flew an aerobatic Pitts Special airplane in air shows; he'd piloted a bobsled in the 1972 Olympics, in Munich, to a bronze medal; in 1979, he'd recovered over ten million dollars in sunken treasure off the Florida Keys; he was on his fifth wife—two of them had been movie actresses; and he'd written several successful country songs that had been recorded by the likes of Willie Nelson and Loretta Lynn.

His latest escapade had made the national news. It involved a daring wing-walk—with no parachute—in the vicinity of several Nashville interstates during rush hour. The doctor was on the wing of a friend's antique Stearman, and they stayed just high enough to be legal. A chase heli-copter had conveniently caught it all for the news.

Sam was a compulsive show-off, and he worked hard at being a caricature of himself.

Visage matched reputation. Weedy salt-and-pepper hair, long and thick, matched a full-face beard and broad eyebrows. Crow's-feet multiplied geometrically when he smiled, highlighting twin-kling eyes with pupils the color of chocolate cake. He looked wild and appeared, at the same time, to be laughing at the world, tempting it to try to get rid of him.

A large potbelly broke through his size XXXL cowboy vest as he swung around the desk to meet Jerry. He laid his chin on his chest and strained his vision through the shaggy eyebrows to say, "Jerry, how, in Jesus, are you? I haven't laid eyes on you since the Halloween party last year, and you and I got schnocked on John Able's back porch. If I recall, Lauren had to pour me in the car with you and drive me home."

"Sam, it's good to see you." Jerry was actually glad to see the psychiatrist, even though it was profes-sionally. Sam was a great guy to be around—always full of anecdotes that effortlessly send his audience into percussive guffaws.

Chin still on his chest to bridge the gap in height, the doctor said, "Lauren told me you've got something really bizarre going. Have a seat." He indicated a comfortable office chair.

"Thanks. I'm not really sure how to go about this. It's been a while since I've been in therapy."

"Well, I wouldn't call it therapy just yet. Start at the top for me."

The psychiatrist let Jerry tell the whole story without interruption. When the musician had finished, Sam said, "How many times now have you written a segment and it's come true?"

"At least five—maybe more."

"Your records from the investigation of your blackouts are at Vanderbilt?"

"Yes. They couldn't find anything to cause them—physically or chemically."

"Sometimes those lesions are practically impossible to see. But they're there all right. Any abnormal behavior, or for that matter, normal behavior, has an endemic effectuality. If something out of the ordinary is taking place in an individual's mind, then the brain has changed in some tiny, bizarre way to cause it. Synapses have been severed, fried, welded; microcosmic quantities of chemical compounds have been altered. Treating the symptoms is another matter. If Vanderbilt did their best and found nothing—physiologically or in the blood work, then the only alternative may be the body's own healing in time. If it's scar tissue causing the problem, it may never dissipate. However, the brain has amazing recuperative powers. If one section refuses to perform ably, then another section will take over its job description. When it heals, it heals slowly—like a wound on a hand or foot. Most nerve cells are never regenerated. However, this is water over the dam. You didn't come here for me to tell you what Vanderbilt has already told you."

"I can deal with the blackouts. It's this other shit that's driving me crazy—all these senseless murders—at least we've got to assume the people are dying. You can't very well cut out an asshole and have the owner still able to play hockey—or bridge."

"Yeah, Lauren told me what was going on."

"It's absolutely bizarre, Sam. It defies all logic unless I'm really killing those people."

Sam leaned back in his desk chair and plopped two scuffed alligator cowboy boots on the desk. "Okay, let's see: You're well alibied during the blackouts; you said that Lauren says she's been with you every time this has happened."

"Yeah, just about."

"Well, obviously, you aren't killing anybody, nor do I believe you're capable of the kinds of psychopathic shit we're seeing in the news media. So . . ."

Jerry interrupted, "But I'm predicting these things, in a way—maybe a different way than your run-of-the-mill psychic does, but nevertheless, I write, they happen!" Jerry squirmed a little in his chair and continued, "Sometimes I have flashes, too, you know, like premonitions, or whatever?"

"Hmmm. That kind of shit always scares the be-jesus outta me. My mother could do it some. Here nor there. This other—writing about the mutilations—there's no way, Little Bubba. Coincidence plays a much larger role on this planet than anyone gives it credit for."

"That's a lot of coincidence, Sam."

"Okay, let me think a minute." The psychiatrist scrunched his eyes and fell silent. With the desk chair protesting in mild, prolonged squeaks, he slowly leaned back farther and farther—so far, in fact, the Jerry was sure the man was going to tip over. Sam's lips were pursed, and he rubbed his chin with his hand—more caricature. Finally, he opened his eyes, straightened up, and said, "Let's do this. Let's perform a scientific experiment. So far, I don't think you have any grounds to go to the police with the fact that you can write about something, then it's going to happen. They won't believe you, even if you give them the time and place. However, if you can document the fact that you wrote it and then it happened, you might be of great assistance to them in solving the whole mess."

"What do I do?"

"Continue writing. I just don't believe you're killing anybody, and I refuse, right now, to start any kind of therapy. Let's approach the problem from an empirical standpoint. Next time you write a big nasty, xerox it immediately, and send it to

me, registered mail. Carolyn will give you the address when you leave. If a murder takes place,
then we have proof you predicted it. And then
we've opened a can of worms that I don't even
want to think about."

Jerry answered him with the first hope he'd realized yet: "Okay."

"Now if it doesn't happen, like I believe it's not
going to happen, because I believe we're dealing
with a bizarre set of coincidences, or something
entirely different, then you're off the hook."

"Sam, that's a great idea. Why didn't I think of
that?"

"Aye, me laddie, that's why I make the big
bucks—fifteen hundred dollars last year." He
broke into another grin.

"And a baby bear don't fart bomb his momma's
face, Sam." Jerry finally managed a grin himself. It
was a well-known fact that Sam made it, and Sam
spent it.

"Send me yer worst, yer swab." He leaned forward, twisted his head, and gave Jerry several exaggerated full-face winks, emulating Captain
Hook's accent and gesture.

III

The next day, Jerry spent most of his time at the word processor in the attic. Creed killed a publishing company executive whose Christian music company had been up to six months late paying for sessions.

Two days later, the news reported the disappearance of Jim Wanderluster the head of JIM Publishing. The JIM stood for Jesus Is Marvelous.

The same day Channel 6 scooped the other stations on *The News At Six* to report another meepbeep had been found on the day after the disappearance—on the desk of one of the JIM Publishing Company's secretaries. When she'd opened the box, she'd thought it was another present from a secret admirer who had been sending her flowers and small porcelain owls. When she discovered the two small slabs of bloody, smelly meat, she'd gone into hysterics and had been taken to the hospital in an ambulance.

The next day, Jerry was back in Wild Sam's office and in such an apparently agitated state that the doctor had given him a tranquilizer. He'd experienced another blackout, and part of the time he'd been alone. He'd had no sessions or appointments, and Lauren hadn't come home until late. There had been no memory of the afternoon or evening.

"Jerry, it may still be coincidence."

"It isn't a coincidence, Sam. Jesus, I wrote specifically about a sacred publishing executive—a sacred publishing company executive's asshole turned up in his own goddamn company. Rightly so, I'll grant you—he was an asshole, but nobody deserves to pay for being a prick with their life!"

"You don't know it was his. There's no proof."

"It's close enough for me."

"Exactly why was—is—this Wanderluster an asshole?"

"Exactly like in the book. He goes ahead and does a big project, and you find out later that the company didn't have any money. The bastard waits until the project starts to bring in money before he pays the musicians. 'God will provide,' and all that shit. Usually, God's a little late."

"Why do you continue to work for him? You don't need the account do you?"

"That's a hell of a good question, Sam. No, I don't need the account. A lot of time a contractor calls, gives you several dates and studios, and doesn't specify what the projects are, or who they're for. You turn up on a date and find out it's someone you didn't want to work for. I've never had the heart to tell the contractor not to call me again for specific companies. It could very well mean losing all the accounts. It's a shortcoming, I guess." To himself, he thought, "And beggars can't be choosers when they enjoy their work and don't get called like they used to."

"I see."

Jerry wrestled in a short bout with the tranquilizer, and in a few minutes his words began to slur. He said, "Ssam, wwhat are we going to do?"

There was no hesitation as Sam said, "We're going to repeat the experiment. Any researcher in his, or her, right mind would repeat the test to see if the results are the same."

"What?"

"Next time you write another murder, you send it to me again. We'll see if the string of coincidences is going to defy all odds."

"Jesus, this ain't no coinc-cccidences anymore." Even more slurred, he continued. "It's g'ddamn dangerous. I think we'd better go to the police. You have the documented ev'dence that what I wrote came true!"

"I have documented evidence of a helluva coincidence. You may be right—there may be something very strange going on, other forces, but I want to test it once more."

"And somebody else dies . . ."

"Maybe. Maybe not. If they do, I still don't believe you're responsible. Let's hang the fleece out again—see what happens."

"Okay, but the blood's on your hands. Goddamn blood's on your hands."

"I can take it. I want you to be exceedingly specific. I mean exceedingly . . ."

The tranquility cleared a little, and Jerry's voice returned more to normal as he said, "I have no sessions the rest of this week. I'd planned to write every day. New York is beginning to pressure me a lot to get the project done. They don't know what's going on down here with all this shit. If they did, they'd probably turn it into a colossal publicity campaign."

"Your publisher, New York?"

"Yeah."

Sam sat up straight and looked directly into Jerry's sleepy eyes. He said, "Write specifically, Little Bubba—document it—every detail."

"Sure." Jerry got up and went to the door with feelings that were mixing with the velocity of a Mixmaster at high speed in spite of the tranquilizer that was now coaxing him to go home and sleep.

"You need a ride home? Carolyn can call a cab."

"No. I'm okay."

The following morning the author was up at five-thirty. A full-scale assault was mounted on the word processor.

CHAPTER FIFTEEN

I

It was cold. There had been frost for the first time the night before. The leaves were turning, falling, metamorphosing the monotonous summer panorama into a magnificent fall kaleidoscope. A light wind was playing the trees like some gargantuan orchestra. Each tree had its own distinct sound, sometimes harmonizing, sometimes discordant with the symphony of the mountain. Had it not been for a late-afternoon shower, it would have been extremely noisy underfoot.

Creed had left the truck in a poorly lit parking lot that belonged to a Brentwood office complex. The hill he'd just climbed, by way of a thick woods, was one of the highest points in Davidson or Williamson counties. Again, fate had smiled on him—provided the perfect answer to a minor irritation—namely, the douche bag Tagglio Khourey whose immortal soul Creed had decided to liberate from the confines of planet Earth.

First of all, the foreigner had no right working in

191

the United States. If the U.S. were to get rid of all the Spics, Chinks, Africans, Aye-rabs, and whoever else had managed to ooze their way onto the shores of life, liberty, and the pursuit of happiness, there would be no unemployment, and the country would be a helluva lot better off.

This bastard was stealing work that belonged to the men who had grown up and had invested their lives here. So what if the working conditions were poor in three-fourths of the rest of the world? Let the lazy bastards do something about it the way the Founding Fathers had in early America. A lot of sweat and blood had been shed to make this country into the land of opportunity, and the goddamn foreigners had been sitting on their asses while it was going on. Now they came over here, legally and illegally, by the millions and took work that rightfully belonged to the heirs of the Americans who had busted their balls and died to get it.

Khourey had been raking in the money, and glory, writing sound scores for some very big movies. When he wasn't doing that, he was arranging national jingles. When he wasn't doing that, he was arranging albums for the biggest names in the music industry. Why the son of a bitch had settled in Nashville was a mystery to Creed, but who better to eliminate one of the country's greatest liabilities than Mr. America, himself—Ronald David Creed—exterminator of un-necessary persons. Khourey's work would then go to someone who had earned the right.

He had got Khourey's address out of the union book. It had been simple to find it on a street map. Driving by in a rental car, he'd discovered it was at the top of a minor mountain that was serviced by a winding road. If the road were not strictly adhered to, it would quickly be determined whether an automobile could truly fly. As in most of Tennessee, guard rails were woefully lacking. The plan came ready-made.

He topped the hill and stood at the edge of the woods. Had anyone been looking, the big man would have been invisible. He was dressed in the usual Woodland camo, his face blackened. There was a small camo fanny pack attached to the web belt that held the camo holster for the Smith and Wesson 9mm automatic. It was loaded with fifteen rounds, and there were three extra clips on the belt in a special pouch.

Legs ached fiercely with fatigue in spite of his being in good shape. This was one hill they would never deface by building houses on it. Creed doubted if mountain goats would even like it.

He had called it perfectly. Khourey's three-stall open garage faced him about seventy yards away, separated from the woods by open lawn and parking area. The parking area was well lighted from a mercury vapor lamp, which exploded with a moderate pop and tinkle of glass from the third shot with a slingshot firing ball bearings. The only worry would be if the place was protected by motion detectors. It was a calculated risk. Besides, the only road up the hill should be visible enough if the cops did come, and the woods were close by if it became necessary for an emergency retreat. There were probably thirty or forty acres of trees and thick brush covering the side of the mountain.

He quickly crossed the open and slipped into the garage. Khourey's big Jaguar was glowering at him in the dark. He quietly popped the hood, stuck a magnetic flashlight to the top of the fender, and located the power brake reservoir. He unscrewed the top and sucked the fluid out with a syringe. The car had been backed into the garage, and brakes would not be needed until Friend Khourey was well on his way down the driveway. By then it would be much too late for the Arab to realize his stopping power had been sucked into Creed's syringe.

Next, he opened the trunk and dug the jack out of the spare tire compartment. He jacked the back end of the car up, got underneath, and with a rubber mallet and ten minutes of exhausting work, chipped the holding pin out of the U-bolt that connected the drive shaft to the rear axle.

"Goddamn thumb," he whispered to himself. He'd broken his thumbnail for the thousandth time. Ever since he was a baby, the nail on his left thumb had grown abnormally fast—sometimes as much as half an inch a week. If he didn't cut it at least every other day, it inevitably got broken.

He replaced the U-bolt's hardened steel pin with

half a dozen glass marbles and sealed them in place with small pieces of putty. The marbles would hold the shaft just enough to get out of the garage and onto the steep driveway. The torque of a couple gear changes would quickly shatter them to dust. The drive shaft would drop away from the rear axle leaving the car effectively in neutral and impossible to slow down by shifting into low.

One more operation remained.

He located the emergency brake cable and cut it in half. The police would know the car had been sabotaged, but that was unavoidable. Khourey was bound to have enemies both in this country and back in Syria. This murder was radically different from the disaster killings. It might not be connected. What the hell if it were.

His only regret was, as on the occasion of Gorman's tragic "suicide," he couldn't remove Khourey's defecation aperture and display it to the world.

He let the car down and replaced the jack exactly as he'd found it. The click from the trunk latch was drowned out by the sound of a car coming up the hill, and it did not sound like it was coming casually. A sixth sense triggered an alarm, and Creed started across the driveway and lawn for the woods. The car cleared the woods that bordered on the street and swung into the driveway with unbelievable quickness. Green strobes exploded into action, and Creed was highlighted in full flight and in the open with about forty yards to go before the woods.

"Hold it! Security!" barked from the cruiser's external speaker.

The car left the driveway and came barreling across the lawn at him. It was evidently from the security company that was connected to Kourney's alarm system.

"Sons of stupid bitches, they're gonna tear the hell out of the fucker's lawn." Creed laughed.

He refused to look at the headlights because it would spoil his night vision once in the woods, but the bastards were getting too close. There were ten yards to go when he heard the blast of a shotgun. Shot sprayed in the tree branches high above his head.

"Stop! That was a warning shot."

"You stupid shits. Do you think it's worth it?"

Without turning to look at them, Creed drew the automatic and emptied fifteen shots into the car, which was no more than twenty yards away as he dived into the woods, laughing almost uncontrollably. He heard the engine goosed as the vehicle slewed around on the wet grass and headed toward the wooded hill at an angle. It didn't slow even slightly as it plowed into the brush, sloshing and bashing its way down the steep hill. There was a hollow thud as it slammed into a tree large enough to halt its flight. Both headlights were smashed, and the sudden stillness and darkness were as welcome to Creed as a beer on a hot, sweaty day. He heard nothing from the men inside and presumed he had either hit them or they had been knocked out by the crash. He had all he could do to keep from bursting into hysterical howls as he made his way slowly back down the hill.

When reported, they would think he was just a run-of-the-mill burglar. They would never thing to check the airworthiness certificate on Khourey's car. Creed would have given a year's pay to have been able to watch it fly off the curve, smashing through the long, loose stone wall that served as a guard rail, then launching its occupant into the screaming solace of empty space.

He wasn't disappointed. The Six O'clock News had some wonderful telephoto shots of the Jaguar lying on its top, blackened by the explosion of a gas tank sparked by impact. They even had shots of a splattered body lying on a bare stretch of rock at the bottom of the valley.

"Damn, Khourey, I sure would have enjoyed cutting out your boz."

He turned the TV off and put Barbra Streisand's Broadway album in the CD player.

"Sing for me, Barby. You know what I want."

II

The registered envelope arrived at Dr. Wild Sam's office as he sat at his desk reading the report of Giacco Arcigo's fiery plunge off the steep hill. Evidently the brakes had failed because there were no skid marks. It would be a day or two before they could recover the car. The world-famous arranger's body had had to be removed by helicopter. The paper said he was working on the sound track for a Richard Thomas movie that had just been filmed locally. Wild Sam hoped it was better than the one they did about Hank Williams Jr.

He didn't open the envelope until Jerry called him late that afternoon. On the phone, the musician sounded like he was in desperate need of more tranquilizers. Sam agreed to see him right away.

Later in his office, after Sam had read the chapter in Jerry's presence, the two men just looked at each other, sitting in silence.

"Alibi?" he asked.

"Ironclad, damn it. This time I was in the middle of a Steve Wariner overdub session. I was at home, and they called me to sub for a ten P.M. session that had already started. The bass singer didn't show up. I had a helluva time getting a baby-sitter for Ginger that fast. I got there only forty-five minutes late, and we were in the studio all night. They had problems with the machine. The producer said he was on a deadline and if we'd stick it out, he'd pay us scale to just sit and wait. I got home at six A.M., and Lauren woke up when I got in bed. She didn't go to work until after Giacco's car went off the cliff and can verify that I was still in bed sleeping. There, by God. That proves it! I couldn't have sabotaged that car because I was with people all night long who can alibi me."

"Then it's not you, Jerry. I never believed it was."

The musician covered his face as the tears and sobs exploded.

Sam let him cry it out, saying nothing, only observing with empathy. When the catharsis was finished, he handed Jerry a box of Kleenex and said, "Who else has seen that chapter?"

Jerry looked at him with bleary eyes and said, "Sam, I haven't shown it to anybody—I haven't even mentioned it to a single soul. I made only one printed copy—you have it. I made two backup copies of the original floppy disk, which is at home locked in my desk. The key is well hidden. I have the backups right here." He patted his attaché. "It would not be possible for anyone on this earth to know what's in that chapter, unless they either burglarized my home and knew how to get into my desk and computer, or they broke into my attaché."

"Did the copy lay around the house or the studio before you mailed it?"

"No. I sealed the copy in the envelope the moment I finished it and went directly to the post office. I was meticulously careful."

"Obviously."

"So what do we do now?"

The psychiatrist was quiet, pensive. Shaking his head, he finally said, "It beats the hell out of me. I guess we'd better go to the police. I'm going with you. Two nut cases are better than one. I don't have any answers. I flat don't know."

"Do you still have the first chapter I sent you by registered mail?"

"Yes. It's unopened."

"Good. That will prove that I have been predicting correctly. Last night's murder will prove that I'm not the murderer because I have an alibi. They've got to believe us."

"I hope so."

The momentum of responsibility had switched from the doctor to the patient. With this ironclad proof that he was not the disaster murderer, Jerry felt somewhat better. However, it only provided more evidence of that frightening little in-law problem that he'd steadfastly refused to consider all along, and he wasn't about to share that minor detail with Sam. In fact, he wasn't about to share that little tidbit with God, Himself.

CHAPTER SIXTEEN

Jerry and Sam had called to get an appointment with a police detective, and it hadn't been easy. Apparently, several hundred other people had called within the last few weeks with certain knowledge of the serial killer. One of them, a prominent Nashville psychic, had shown up with a complete newscam crew.

However, the two bottom lines were: Homicide was tired of cranks but had to check them all out; and in spite of Fawley's brilliant powers of deduction, nobody had the slightest clue who the real killer was—if there was a killer. There were still no bodies to be reconciled with the last few inches of the alimentary canals in the boxes labeled "POLICE."

The Justice Center switchboard had transferred Jerry to Missing Persons; Missing Persons had transferred him to Homicide; Homicide had transferred him twice, and after a total of eight minutes of being on hold, he had finally got to talk to

Detective Walter Klinghafen, who actually was not working on the case but would meet with Jerry and his doctor to discuss the information they had to offer. His office was on the third floor.

When Jerry and Sam asked for him, they were pointed toward a desk at the far end of the room with a, "The guy with the schnoz behind the paperwork." The desk's perimeter was covered with stacks of files. The working area was filled with assorted forms and typewritten papers, a couple of books and several stacks of computer read-outs.

The detective did not acknowledge them until they were standing directly in front of him, and Jerry said, "Detective Klinghopper?"

Klinghafen fingered his place in a file and closed it, looking up at the same time. Jerry estimated the detective was about six feet, medium build. His face, all but obliterated by an enormous, bulbous nose, was pockmarked badly. Dark networks of veins appeared sporadically across the nose and cheeks, and fanned outward toward jaw angles. He took the glasses off and said, "Klinghafen. You must by Mr. Cayce."

"Yes. This is Doctor . . ."

"Bruckstein." The detective broke into a grin and stood, losing his place in the file. "Wild Sam Bruckstein. It's a pleasure to meet you, Doctor. I've admired your style for years." He shook hands with both men.

Sam grinned back and said, "I'm not sure if that's a compliment, considering some of the more stupid things I've done, but I'll accept it as one."

He motioned the doctor to one chair, stood and walked over to the next desk, and brought another chair for Jerry.

"Okay. Let me explain the department's lack of jumping at the offer to help. We've been inundated with *help* for weeks now, and so far, none of it's been worth a hoot."

Sam answered him, Jerry having been relegated to the position of semi-obscurity. "I think this may be of interest. Just how, neither Jerry or I really know, at this point."

He handed the opened registered mail envelope to the detective, still holding onto the unopened first envelope Jerry had sent him.

"Note the date. It will become very important."

The cop took the envelope, noted the date, then pulled out the sheaf of printed sheets.

"What is it?"

Sam turned to Jerry and said, "Jerry, why don't you try to explain."

Jerry had been watching the detective with interest. He should have been scared out of his wits, but for some reason he wasn't. With a firm voice, he said, "I'll make it short. I'm in the music business. I'm writing a novel about a psychotic musician who is killing off his competition, cutting out their anuses, and sending them to the police."

Klinghafen interjected, acidly, "A takeoff on what's been going on around here. A little opportunistic, isn't it?" If it hadn't been for Sam, he'd have thrown the musician out.

"No."

The officer perked up at the conflagration, his disgust unchanged.

"You see, I started writing the novel before all this started to happen. The reason we're here is going to shock the piss out of you, once you see the proof."

"Proof?"

Jerry continued, "I concoct a specific murder, a specific situation—say a chapter in the novel where an arranger gets murdered and the killer sends the by-product of his radical surgery to the police in a small cardboard box. A few days later, you have a missing person, and a little cardboard box labeled 'POLICE' shows up."

"Proof?" He was interested now, but skeptical.

"It's in your hand. The last two murders I've conceived of, I've documented by sending them to Doctor Bruckstein by registered mail. He opened the one you have in your hand to read it. The other one, as you can see"—Sam handed him the other envelope—"is unopened. Note the date. You open it, you read it. You'll see that I wrote about someone like Jim Wanderluster of JIM music getting killed before he turned up missing, and you found another asshole in a box."

"Is this for real?" The detective looked at Jerry, then at Sam.

Sam answered, "I'm afraid the boy's got his ducks in a row." He continued, "The opened envelope's a chapter about a big-shot arranger from another country whose car is sabotaged and takes him off a mountain curve."

"Jesus, Giacco Arcigo—two days ago." He looked again at the envelope's documented date of three days before.

"Ehyut."

They had snared the detective's interest now. His gaze left the chapter in his hand, and for the first time, he really looked at Jerry. "Obviously, you have an ironclad alibi or you wouldn't be here."

Jerry answered, "Ironclad. I was in the studio all night working on a Steve Wariner project. We didn't leave the studio until six A.M. I went straight home to bed with my wife, Laura. The paper said Arcigo was killed at eight-thirty. A neighbor saw him go off the curve. There would have been no way I could have driven thirty miles, sabotaged his car, and got home by six-thirty. Lauren was with me until she left for work at eight-thirty."

"Very interesting."

Jerry continued, "Let me qualify something. You'll find out anyway."

"Yeah?"

"For a year, or so, I've had a problem with blackouts. I come back to the real world a few hours later and have no memory of what's happened."

"Are you an alcoholic, Mr. Cayce?"

"No. They're not alcohol induced."

"What about drugs in the past?"

"No. I've never done drugs other than doctor's prescriptions, and I'm not just saying that to protect myself in front of a police officer."

Sam interjected, "Detective, we think Jerry has some type of rare epilepsy. So far, the medical tests have not come up with a handle, but then there are scores of diseases for which we don't have handles."

"I see. Go on, Mr. Cayce."

"Well, there have been some incidences when I was in a blackout the night before you received your little presents. Most of the times my wife can alibi me. There are a couple I don't have alibis for."

"Really?"

Sam interjected, "I don't believe Jerry's capable of killing anyone, Detective, even if he did not have an alibi."

Jerry added, "You'd be suspicious if I could account for every single incident, wouldn't you?"

"Yeah, I guess you're right—if the victim was actually relieved of his south end the day, or night, before we received them. It's possible that the

meat could have been stored for a while in a refrigerator before being dumped on us while an
alibi was established." He was watching Jerry
carefully for a reaction. There was none. He finally continued, "However, we believe they were
fresh. The meat would have to be stored at pre-
cisely the right temperature, and that's difficult
without a special refrigerator. So, I guess if your
alibis were too pat, I would be a little suspicious."

Jerry simply said, "Thank you."

The detective scratched the side of his magnificent nose for a few seconds, then said, "Okay, you
have an alibi. Obviously, you've told somebody, or
someone is reading those chapters and then, for
some bizarre reason, is carrying out the murders.
Have you told anybody what you're writing?"

"Not a soul."

"Who else has read your manuscript?"

"No one that I know of." Jerry looked down at
the pile of paper in the middle of the desk, then
back up at the policeman apologetically.

"No one could get their hands on it without
your knowing it?"

"It's possible. But it wouldn't be easy. I usually
have a copy of the manuscript and floppy disks
with me when I leave the house. They're in my
attaché—in case I get a chance to work on them.
Some of the places I work have PCs, and they let
me use them during breaks. If they don't, I write
in longhand."

"Another copy of the manuscript? Backup disks?"

"Yes, at the house locked in the desk."

"Could someone be getting into your house unnoticed?"

"I sincerely doubt it. There's a burglar alarm. It's always on if Lauren and I aren't home. Anyway, why would someone want to read what I've written, then carry out the action? What purpose would it serve?"

"Stranger things have happened. Someone might want to discredit you—have you discredit yourself. Maybe someone doesn't want you to have the book published."

"That's a helluva bloody way to keep a guy from publishing a book. What difference should my book make to anyone? I mean, who cares?"

"You don't have any enemies who would want to deprive you of fame and fortune?"

"Hell, no."

Sam interrupted, "Jerry, could you have shown your work to someone during one of your blackouts and not remembered?"

Jerry answered instantly, "I've thought of that. Each of the blackouts I've had, that have been during one of the crucial times when they've found another asshole, I've either been with Lauren or by myself. I would have had to make a special effort to tell someone. You know, go to somebody's house, or phone them. 'Hi Dave, I just wrote another murder that the psycho commits with a pickle fork and two tins of shoe polish.' It doesn't make sense that I would do something like that when I feel so strongly about doing it in real life."

"Laura's your wife?" the detective asked.

"Right. Loving, stunning to look at, a first-class mother, talented at what she does—a remarkable woman. *Sometimes it would be wonderful to be out of all this; to just to be normal. Unburdened.*"

"And you haven't discussed any of your writing even with your wife?"

Jerry continued, "Sometimes we'll discuss ideas. I mean, it's only natural to bounce things off someone. Sometimes she has some really good suggestions. As far as her knowing exactly what I've written, she doesn't."

"Mr. Cayce, please forgive me, but I've got to ask. Your wife has alibied you for your blackouts, and she would have access to the manuscript. Is there any reason on God's green earth that she would want to do these horrible things?"

Jerry should have been upset, but for some reason, not understood, he was resolved.

"I understand, but no, sir. She would have no motive whatsoever. *What he doesn't know won't hurt him. That horrible business when she and Larry were in high school* ... Oh, God—if they find out." His heart began to thump in fear, but he managed to hide it.

The detective rubbed his nose some more, thinking. Then he said, "Did you ever consider putting a halt on the writing for a couple of months to see if the murders stop?"

Jerry looked down at the desk, then into the cop's eyes directly once more and said, "Yeah. I stopped for about a month. But the mutilations kept turning up anyway. The problem is, there's as much killing in the book as there was in the old Italian Westerns—enough to keep the thing going for a while if the killer wanted to document every single one. So far, he's skipped around. Not every murder I've written about has been copycatted. I'm sure he's smart enough to know that he couldn't kill that many times without screwing up and getting caught. He's picking and choosing and doing it carefully."

Sam interjected again. "What kind of stuff remains that hasn't been fulfilled, at least to our knowledge? You know, he could be doing all of them, and we just haven't found out."

Jerry answered emphatically. "No. I firmly believe he'd have to devote himself full-time—give up his day job. This isn't the kind of guy who would go to the trouble of having all that fun and not let us know about it."

"You may have a point there."

The musician continued, "Let's see . . . the killer—his name is Creed—goes on a spree and kills three musicians in two days."

"Any others?" Klinghafen had been taking notes furiously. He had stopped and unconsciously begun to twirl the pencil in his fingers like a majorette twirls a baton.

Jerry met his eyes and said, "Well, enough to keep thing hopping right along. We certainly don't want the reader to get bored." Jerry continued. "There are some flashbacks in Creed's life. He's been killing since he was six years old. He pushed a three-year-old into a swimming pool because the kid wouldn't quit crying."

"Jesus. A mean son of a bitch. I hope we don't have one of those for real."

Sam answered, "I'm afraid we may have, Detective. Mass murderers are few and far between, but when they come along, they're hard to catch, and they don't feel sorry for what they're doing."

The detective glanced toward the window. A flock of pigeons had just made a pass at the building before swerving away. His gaze went down to the river. One of the paddle wheelers was chugging against the current. Finally he said, "So there's enough ammunition to keep him busy for a long time to come, even if you stop writing?"

Jerry answered, "I'd have to quit permanently—trash the book. I would be willing to do that if it would stop the killing, but there's no guarantee that the killer wouldn't continue. As long as I'm not doing it . . . Damn it, it's a good book—and the publisher is getting impatient. I really need to continue and finish."

"In spite of worldwide publicity giving away your plot, they still want it now?"

"We've talked. They still want it—worse than ever."

The detective answered once more, "Yeah, I see the point. Well, it's a puzzle to me, gentlemen. Let me keep these chapters. I'll talk it over with John Fawley. He's the head of the task force that's trying to find the killer."

Jerry quickly yelped, "Fawley . . . John Fawley?"

"Yeah. He's an inspector. Why, do you know him?"

"When did he start on the case?"

The detective answered, "About three months ago, when the shit hit the fan—when all the musicians really started turning up missing."

Jerry went on. "The inspector in my book who is the head of the task force to find the killer? His name is Joe Farley—John Fawley—Joe Farley? I had Farley on paper five months ago."

The detective and the doctor were both visibly shocked. Sam was the first to say, "That's a fright, Jerry, but chances are, you picked his name up unconsciously in the paper or TV."

"I doubt it, Doctor," the detective said. "The lieutenant was just transferred here from Denver three months ago on loan—he's a specialist in serial murders. That's as close as two names can get without being the same."

Before Jerry and Sam had left the building, Klinghafen was on the phone patched through to Fawley's car radio. "John, I need to see you as soon as possible. It's about your serial killer case. You're not going to believe . . ."

In the car, Sam turned to Jerry and said, "Jerry, how much do you know about Lauren's past?"

"You mean the trouble she and Larry got into in high school. That it?"

"Yeah. She ever tell you about it?"

"Not in detail. She doesn't like to talk about it. She only mentioned that her mother was murdered."

"She was not only murdered, she was butchered—mutilated horribly. Did you know they were almost certain it was Larry? They'd suspected him of mutilating animals for years."

"Yeah, I knew about all that before I married Lauren. She told me they'd gone to a movie. They came home and found the police rolling their mother out in a body bag."

"She and Larry were incredibly close. Twins usually are."

"They're still close."

"Do you have any idea how close they've always been, Jerry?"

"What do you mean?"

"The scar on Lauren's stomach. She ever tell you about that?"

"No. She said it was appendix or something."

"In a way it was. I'm not telling you anything that isn't public knowledge or that hasn't been written up extensively. That scar came from an appendectomy, all right—Larry's appendectomy!"

"What do you mean?"

"When Larry was seventeen years old, he and some friends were camping in the mountains. He got an acute attack of appendicitis, and had it not been for a doctor who was out hiking with his family . . . With no anesthetic, the doctor operated on him with a hunting knife and sewed him up with a fishhook and fishline. Had they waited until Larry got to a hospital, the appendix would have ruptured and he would have died."

"And . . ."

"Lauren still has her appendix. At the same time the doctor was operating on Larry, Lauren was sleeping on the living room sofa. She woke up soaked in blood. There was a serious wound on her stomach, and they had to rush her to the emergency room. It was the exact same wound that the doctor gave Larry with the hunting knife."

Jerry was openmouthed. He barely whispered, "My God. Is that possible?"

"Things like that happen occasionally. It's a hysterical manifestation through telepathy—well documented."

"She never said anything about it."

"You know that they both were under my care for several years?"

"Yes. She said it was something to do with the emotional problems that came from their father's death. He was on a business trip when his plane crashed off the coast of Australia. They never found his body. She said the death of her parents were one of the reasons she went into thanatological and geriatric counseling."

"Yes."

"So, what were they being treated for?"

"Jerry, I can't reveal that kind of confidentiality without Lauren's permission. The reason I brought it up is because I think you should ask her. It probably has no bearing on all these murders, but you should at least know the possibilities—It's Larry I'm thinking about."

Jerry mentally kicked his brain. To himself, he said, *"Maybe it's time I got my head out of my meepbeep and faced reality."*

CHAPTER SEVENTEEN

I

Jerry had arrived home about four-thirty after dropping Sam off at his office. Feelings were mixed. He felt a burden had been lifted from his shoulders, but there were so many unresolved problems. Also, he was beginning to see the development of something that, for years, he had dreaded he would have to face.

Lauren was already home. He could just see her blond head through the kitchen window. She was wearing pigtails. She must have been in front of the sink working on supper.

As he entered the back door into the kitchen, she turned, smiled, and said, "Okay, Sherlock. How'd it go? Give." She was wearing a pink sweat suit. Pink always made him a little crazy, and she knew it.

Jerry wrapped his arms around her from behind, before answering, and continued to spoon his body against her. Maybe love would stop the madness.

217

"Not bad. You'll notice I'm here, not in jail. They're as baffled as we are." He proceeded to give her the details. She continued to clean vegetables in the sink as he nuzzled her cheek.

When he had finished, he summarized by saying, "So, they think someone is getting into the house and looking at the manuscript."

Lauren said immediately, "That's insane. We don't know anybody who'd want to do something that horrible. Even if we did, how in the world could they pull it off?"

Jerry continued, "I have no idea, but it might not be entirely out of the question. How many people have keys to the house and alarm besides you and me?"

She thought for a minute, placed another foil-wrapped potato onto a pan with four others, then answered, "Three. The Hobkirks have one . . ." The alarm system was notorious for being set off by thunderstorms. Rather than let it ring for hours, the next-door neighbors would investigate and turn it off. Colin Hobkirk was an FBI agent. His wife, Marie, owned a travel agency. "Oh, by the way, they're coming over for a barbecue tonight." She turned back to him with a questioning face. "You hadn't forgotten, had you?" The Hobkirks lived across the hedge in the rustic New England saltbox next door.

"I had, but it doesn't matter. It'll be just what I need. Drink a little beer . . . Maybe Colin will

have some ideas about me and our friend the serial killer." He paused. "What are we having?"

"Filet mignon and baked potatoes, salad—you
get to cook."

"Great. Where's the beer?" He had opened the
refrigerator. "And who else has keys?"

"Larry has a set, of course," she answered, "and
it's in a cooler on the back deck. Bring me one
too, please. I gave him the extra set a long time
ago so he could feed Dolby when we're at the
lake." The cat preferred a little loneliness to the
two-hour ride to the lake.

"Yeah," he answered as he exited into the den
on his way to the deck. "Where'd you get the
steaks?"

Lauren hadn't heard the question over the water running in the sink and hollered to him, "If
anything ever happens to us, he would be the one
to look after the house."

As Jerry returned, he repeated the question.
"Did you get the steaks at Ivey's? You know there
are none better."

He twisted the caps off and poured Lauren's
into a lager glass. His he drank from the bottle.

"Of course."

"Hey, did Larry every find out who scratched his
boat up?"

"I didn't know it was scratched up."

"Yeah. Last time I saw it, the bottom was all
banged up."

Jerry's mind returned to the real question he wanted to ask.

She shocked him by replying, "We were in the medical journals around the world for a while."

Jerry didn't follow and said, "Pardon me?"

She was cleaning and cutting up the salad vegetables. "When we were kids, Larry and I were the only case on record of twins both being diagnosed as schizophrenic. Mine went away, he still takes medication."

She had anticipated him and answered the question before he could ask it. Jerry often wondered if Lauren entertained premonitions the way he did. She had never admitted to it, but occasionally she did shock him. The telepathic ability with her twin was certainly a given.

She began to toss the salad and continued as if nothing had happened. "Okay, keys . . . Ellen has a set."

"That's right. I'd forgotten about that."

Three days a week, a maid came to clean. The same lady had been working for them for two years. Her husband was a fine guitarist and had been trying to break into the recording business for several years. Unfortunately, his talent accompanied an attitude problem that had kept him from ever making it among the session players. Instead of trying to get a job on the road, or starting a new career, he had sat around the house and grown bitter. The family had come from Brooklyn, and every time Jerry saw him he was continually threatening to move back.

"Any more?" He bit into a celery stalk.

She turned, a little puzzled, and said, "You know there is a fourth set. When your mom died, she had one, and I don't know whatever became of it. That was, what . . . almost four years ago? I suppose it's packed away in all that stuff that's in storage." She was punching the steaks full of holes with a meat fork, preparing to marinate them with teriyaki sauce. Turning around to face him, there was a puzzled look on her face as she said, "Wait a minute! Jerry, didn't we give some of those things to that couple whose house burned down last year? You know, the one the union was collecting for?"

"Yeah. The wife was doing a little arranging for *Music City Tonight*. She'd had a tough time getting work—it's hard enough for a man. Her husband had just gotten out of prison if I remember right—some pair, weren't they?"

"Very strange."

"I heard someone say they were leaving town for good."

Jerry continued munching, "You know, it's not outside the realm of possibility that someone who knows who we are found the keys even before we gave all that stuff away."

"I guess," she agreed, and started mixing the salad dressing.

II

The evening was a relaxing success. Jerry asked Colin about the FBI's reaction to the boxes labled "POLICE." The agent said the Investigative Support Unit at Quantico was assisting Metro with tentative psychological profiles but that they were as mystified as the police. There were no bodies. Colin had not been assigned personally to work on the case, so he wasn't aware of the details. When Jerry explained the way he'd been documenting the killings before they'd happened and that the police were aware of this, Colin was astonished. He could give Jerry no advice other than to find the lost keys.

The Hobkirks left early, and while Lauren put the finishing touches on the kitchen cleaning, Jerry lounged in the recliner in the den. His mind went to its usual haunt—why couldn't he get the kind of work he used to have? Maybe he shouldn't have let a lot of the things happen to him that he had—companies and producers steamrolling him and taking advantage of him.

Most of it was the same story: a would-be artist or a fledgling jingle company would ask him to work dirt cheap or on spec. He'd do it, working hard to make the best product possible. Then as soon as the artist had hit it big, or the jingle company came up with a McDonald's, they'd dump him for another arranger—one who was more contemporary.

Several producers had run up a giant tab for his work—as much as ten thousand dollars on a couple of occasions. "Jerry, just as soon as we get paid, you'll be the first to get a check." But as soon as they got paid, the money had gone elsewhere—sometimes into their own pockets. They knew he would never sue them.

Lauren had implored him over and over to stick up for his rights, to fight, make a fuss. But he just wasn't any good at it, preferring to let it go rather than initiate a confrontation.

"How much you make doesn't always determine how successful you are, Lauren."

"Jerry, that's easy for you to say because you were born into a wealthy family. You work for self-satisfaction—because you love music, not necessarily to make money. To some people, money is everything, and they'll do anything to get it. They don't mind lining their own pockets by stealing from somebody like you who'll work for nothing."

"Well, I know it's not right. But they'll get theirs. It'll come back around." But it never had. To a lot of the people he'd helped become successful, Jerry Cayce was merely over-the-hill history.

They were, indeed, assholes. The ones who had been murdered had finally got what they deserved. Bastards! He would have enjoyed cutting out

some of their assholes—make them eat it before
they died!

III

"So we've established, once and for all, that the
missing people were not taken at any special time of
the month. He's not on a moon cycle?"

"Right."

"And there's no common denominator with any of
them as far as a health club, grocery store, instru-
ment repair business ...? He's gotta be picking his
victims from somewhere besides the Sears catalog."

"It's all been walked, cross-checked. Posey,
Sanderson, and Tremont have been tramping the
streets for weeks. The only thing in common is the
musicians involved and that most of them belong to
the unions."

Tony Jeeters was sitting in front of Farley's desk
with an open file in his lap, a calendar in one hand
and a cup of coffee in the other. The investigation's
fatigue was evident on the faces of both men. It had
dragged on for months without a single break.

Farley was looking out the window. A tug was
muscling four sand barges up to the Ingram warf.
Most of the soil in Middle Tennessee was clay based.
In order for the construction companies to manufac-

ture cement, sand had to be barged from Kentucky and beyond.

Farley's glasses magnified dark circles laced with yellow beneath his eyes. The rainy-day light from the window behind him bathed the room in a pewter glow. It highlighted the gray in his hair, making him appear even older than he felt. Aches and occasional pain stabs from the accumulative lack of sleep harassed him without mercy. At the moment, he was homesick for his wife and two teenage daughters. It would pass. After all those years of marriage, it would just take a lot of time.

"Joe, I may have something!"

Detective Aaron Delaney barged into Farley's office without bothering to knock. He was obviously excited over something. Farley and Jeeters looked at him with a hint of hope. Anything was better than going over and over the same old files in hope of something that had been missed.

"It may be what we've been looking for—and then it may not."

"Beggars can't be choosers, Aaron."

Farley opened the lower desk drawer and took out a bottle of Windex and a roll of paper towels. Then he removed his glasses and proceeded to clean them. He always tried to give the impression of insouciance whenever he became excited. In his mind it kept him one step above the other men, looking down— exactly where a supervisor should be.

"Yeah, well, this one guy—musician I questioned—

Ron Creed—nasty fellow and very uncooperative—took me six or seven times before I even found him home. Big. Looked part Indian or something."

"Yeah?"

"Well, I asked him if he was into guns. He said no. The reason I asked him was I could smell what could have been gun-cleaning solvent—like we use—Hoppe's?"

"Yeah."

"He piqued my curiosity—if he was cleaning guns, why would he deliberately lie about it?"

"Good word that 'piqued,' eh, Joe?"

"Jeeters, hush! Give the guy a break. Good question, Aaron. Go on." Farley had finished the glasses and gave Delaney his full attention.

Delaney continued, "So I ran the guy's name through the Tennessee ATF database, and, sure enough, he'd just bought a new Smith and Wesson nine millimeter a few months ago from Briley's."

"Go on."

"It gets better. I ran his name through every database I could get my hands on from traffic to season tickets at Vanderbilt—took me half the day. Surprise, surprise. His name just kept dancing its way right onto my screen."

"You've got my undivided attention, Aaron." Farley began to feel the suspense building, and it was the first pleasant feeling he'd experienced in a long time.

"You know the IRS agent who disappeared?"

"Go on . . ."

"Creed was one of his customers. An unsatisfied one I found out when I called over there. It seems he dumped the agent's computer on the floor and got away with it. The man was terrified, wouldn't let anyone file charges."

"And all these years I thought Uncle Sam's finest weren't scared of anything. What a letdown. I'm going home and cry."

"Save it, Jeeters. You may not have to. Our friend, Ronald David Creed was involved in a traffic accident with a sixteen-year-old-girl—the one who disappeared leaving only her keys behind."

"Becky Aldrich."

"Yup. And it still gets better."

Farley stood up and said, "Help me here, Aaron. Let it be what we need it to be. I'm asking you real hard."

"Try this—this boy is an arranger, a keyboard player, and a singer—three for three; and his work dues at all three unions have doubled and tripled since all the musicians have disappeared. He's benefiting big time!"

"I'm tempted to send a SWAT team. If he's our guy, he is a total psycho. However, all we've got is circumstantial, and the chief would blow a mother board if this isn't our man and it hits the media that we took him with a SWAT team. Take two men and two cars of uniforms, and bring this guy's ass down here. Let's steamroll him in front of the mirror—

227

three men hosing him hard—see why he lied. We're due for a break."

"I'm gone!"

IV

Creed sat at a battered table in a metal chair. The room looked exactly like it did in all the movies and television, complete with a smudged one-way mirror. Farley, looking old and used, stood in one corner of the room.

Delaney, much younger, had a thick file in his hand. He looked the big man squarely in the eye and said, "Mr. Creed, you do understand that even though we are only questioning you, you have the right to have a lawyer present?"

Creed glared at him and said, "Cut the bullshit. What do you want?"

Farley asked, *"Mr. Creed, would you like to go out on the balcony awhile?"*

Creed ignored him, thought to himself, "How'd you like this goddamn chair shoved up your skinny twat ass?"

Delaney proceeded to ask several of the same questions he had asked Creed before. Creed was noticeably petulant in his answers.

". . . You said you knew Bartholomew, Joince, Crouser, Dearsley . . ."

"Goddamn it!" Creed finally exploded. "If your memory sucks that badly, then you need a head transplant. All these answers are obviously in the report in your hand. What the hell do you really want to know? You're boring the shit out of me!"

Delaney put the report back into the file and placed it on the table.

"All right. You lied to me about not owning any guns. Why?"

Creed fired back with venom. "I may have lied to you about a lot of other things. It's one of the rights guaranteed by the Constitution, isn't it?"

"Why are you so uncooperative. You hiding something?"

"Oh, Sweetiz Jessiz! I knew you'd find out. All right—I confess: I'm the guy who shot John Kennedy. Sorry, but I missed Jackie. I confess it all. You got me. Now, if you're through with your little sandpaper circle jerk, I'm going home!"

"Mister, you're not going anywhere until we get some answers." Farley had opened his mouth for only the second time.

Creed turned to him and spat, "Then you bastards better send for room service, because we're in for a helluva long night."

The younger detective fired questions at him for the next hour, pacing up and down the room, hoping to hit a nerve. Farley remained standing quietly in the background as Delaney ran the gamut: alibis, relationship with the missing and murdered musicians, the benefits from the deaths of his competitors, and why he had lied about the guns. They'd run a routine financial query on the big man, and Delaney delved into it in great detail. He wanted to know why, with that kind of money, Creed was working at all; why he came to Nashville; where the money had come from; did he run dope?

The whole time, the big man stared at the far wall, arms in his lap, feet flat on the floor, never once opening his mouth. Only at one point did he move. He pulled out his fingernail clippers and cut his thumbnail.

At one point, the older officer said, *"Mr. Creed. How are you doing in there? Why won't you ever talk to us? We know you're thinking in there. Do you realize how long it's been?"* He squatted in front of the frozen man to intercept the unfocused stare.

At ten-thirty P.M., Creed looked at his watch, got to his feet, and said quietly, "Either charge me with something, or I'm walking out of here. You lay a finger on me, and I'll plaster you all over the goddamn wall."

They let him go—not from fear, but because they had no authority to hold him.

Within two hours, another anus was found, this time, on the front seat of a police cruiser parked in the Parking For Booking Only zone next to the Justice Center's side entrance. There was no box.

The body was never found, but the mangled piece

of meat was unmistakably identified as belonging to Patrolman John Trubles. His name tag was pinned to the skin.

The next day at eleven A.M., it was learned that one of the night-shift patrolmen had seen a big man casually walking down the sidewalk on Second Avenue—about a hundred yards from the entrance. He had dark hair and was dressed like Creed. He'd remembered the man, because, although he wasn't sure, he thought the guy had given him the finger.

Farley took no chances after not finding the musician home. He issued an All Points Bulletin for Ronald David Creed—believed to be armed and extremely dangerous.

He was a little late. By nine A.M., Creed had emptied his bank accounts of over three hundred thousand dollars. The cash, in tens, twenties, and fifties, had gone into a waterproof box. There was still a very sizable Swiss account they'd never find.

His pack contained the finest bare necessities money could buy—Thinsulate winter sleeping back, Gortex-lined insulated camo winter garments. The jeep had been paid for in cash, and the tags issued to a name that was backed up by false identification. Creed had several false IDs that were legitimate. He'd learned how to get them years ago from a *Soldier Of Fortune* magazine.

The big man had prepared for this day for years. And he had prepared very well. Now the real fun could begin. Damn, he was looking forward to this.

CHAPTER EIGHTEEN

I

Most of the russet leaves were on the ground. There had been frost for a week straight, but the November days were in the fifties and sixties. Creed was enjoying the wilderness immensely.

He'd bought the one hundred twenty acres bordering the Cheatham County Game Reserve four years before under another fake identity, just in case. It was a good place to hunt, although the big man had outgrown killing animals years before. People were much more satisfying. If he'd needed the meat it would have been different, but to kill for sport turned him off. Grandfather had taught him that senselessly taking something you couldn't put back was wrong.

"You can replace a burned home or a wrecked automobile, Ronnie—in fact, you can replace almost anything with enough money and hard work. But once you snuff out the life of any living creature—even a cricket or a spider, you can't put it back. Life is sacred, son. We have no right to take it needlessly."

When it came to humans, "Yeah, but sometimes a man's gotta do what a man's gotta do, Grandpa—may you rest in peace."

He kept the cabin stocked with enough food to last several months, and during the second year had trucked in a five-hundred-gallon tank of kerosene for heat, pulling it off the truck bed onto a cradle using the truck's winch. The sight and smell of a wood fire could easily give him away. There was also a mountain of ammunition buried beneath the floor.

During hunting season each year, he'd come out to stay and walk around the woods carrying the gun. There was always a spot on a tree to shoot at. In several places, he'd placed tin cans on bushes.

The old barn behind the cabin had been full of hay bales, although Creed had never figured out why someone had gone to all the trouble to bring them all the way out there in the woods. They proved useful because he covered the jeep with them so any snooping hunters wouldn't see it. He'd posted the land to try to keep them away, but it didn't always work.

About three months after he'd been hiding out, an astute real estate agent had notified the police that the man who had bought the place several years before, looked a lot like the sketches in the paper they kept showing of the man who might be the serial killer.

When they came for him, he had been expecting them. The real estate agent, seeking some free advertising, had notified the TV and radio stations. Creed had been listening to the radio, as usual, for news and had heard the whole thing.

When he finally left the cabin, he could hear them coming over a mile away. Over the four years he'd had the place, he'd made numerous caches of supplies. Some were buried in caves, some were scattered around the woods, buried beneath a special pattern of pine trees he'd planted to indicate a cache.

They had brought dogs, but the animals had rebelled in pain after sniffing a trail of sustained red pepper. There were enough swift-running bedrock creeks and rocky terrain to throw off a master tracker, and Creed certainly wasn't stupid enough to put socks over his boots to try to hide the print—an expert tracker could easily recognize the weave in the socks. Walking backward wouldn't work either. The deep heel print and light toe print were dead giveaways.

The only real problem was dodging the night helicopters with their infrared scopes. However, the big man had carefully treated his clothes with the same chemical the army did to prevent detection. If they found him, they were going to work harder than they ever had before. He had been taught by his grandfather, the old *cherchinka*—there was no one better. If Ronald David Creed chose to remain invisible, to anyone searching for him it would seem like he'd vanished from the face of the earth.

II

He was just an old drifter, a drunk, an alumnus of Salvation Army Service Centers from El Paso to Bangor. It had been oppressively hot for a whole week. Summer night air, globbed and sticky as oatmeal, poured trouble into a silver chalice of boredom and served it in surfeit. Black men had no business here. It'd be doing the county a service.

"Hey, mister. Got a jug here. You want a hit?"

The drunk had just finished a quart of Pearl and was feeling no pain. It was a good thing.

She was doing the laundry in the garage when she felt him tremble with excitement, saw him pull the knife. Her mother discovered her rolling around on the cement floor hands squeezed between her legs. Afterward, the woman would swear her fifteen-year-old daughter was having an orgasm.

III

"C'mon, Ginger. You're going to make us late."

"I can't get this stupid barrette to close!"

The entire family had been looking forward to the Ice Capades. Every time they came to town, it was a must-see on the Cayce's list of *Things To Do.*

"Do you think Goofy will be there this year, Mommy?"

"I don't know, honey. He was really neat wasn't he?" Lauren closed the barrette and adjusted it in the little girl's thick, blond hair.

The year before, Goofy had skated over to Ginger's rink-side seat and given her a high five. Lauren had marveled at how the kids knew how to do that at such an early age. Goofy had occupied the center of conversation for the next week.

Ten minutes later, the Cayces were on the Interstate headed toward the heart of town.

IV

Two hours and forty-five minutes earlier, at 4:25 in the afternoon, John Ball had pulled up to the pumps at the 76 Truck Stop in Jackson, Tennessee. He had been up at 5:00 A.M. on the previous day in order to drive seventy miles to the wire manufacturing plant in Barstow, California, where he operated a cutter. At 3:15 P.M. he had been called away from his machine to receive an emergency phone call. It was his younger sister in Tennessee, and she was in tears. Their mother had had a stroke, she was in University Hospital in Knoxville, and she was not expected to live very long. John and his mother had not been close for years, but here was a genuine quest—a family emergency—the kind of situation where logic and common sense are set on the back burner, and a man does what he has to do. John had immediately left work to begin the tortuous drive across seven states. Fortunately, it was all interstate, in fact the same interstate—I-40—for the entire trip.

The motel down the street from the truck stop looked tempting beyond belief, but John knew he would never forgive himself if he was sleeping while his mother passed on and he was only a few hours away.

"The worst is over, Johnny, my boy. You can do the rest with your hands tied behind your back."

He had the restaurant waitress fill his thermos with black coffee while he made his way to the trucker's fuel counter where, close by, there should be a sliding-glass-door refrigerator with the "to go" sandwiches packed in their sealed, hard-plastic wedges. He grabbed a half-dozen tuna salad and pimento cheese on white and a large bag of potato chips.

By the time John had reached Nashville, the coffee was gone. This time it hadn't done much good. He'd fought sleep seriously for the last two hours. He had tried rolling down the window to stick his head into the slipstream. He'd tried opening his mouth wide and baring his teeth to let the cold air flow into his mouth and over his gums. With the radio turned up as loud as it would go, he had sit-

danced on the seat while he sang at the top of his voice to a new hit by Travis Tritt and an old hit by Janie Fricke. Twice he'd nodded off and had caught himself when the car hit the rough shoulder of the interstate. It had frightened him badly and the adrenaline had held out for fifteen minutes each time. He knew he should stop. But what would the family say if they found out he was holed up in a motel while his mom . . .

One of the most amazing things about life on planet Earth is the tenuousness of it. One second a person is breathing, metabolizing food and oxygen, firing off millions of pulses of electrical current, and producing hundreds of chemical changes. The next instant the stray bullet, or the unseen plummeting airplane, or John Ball, in his tan Chevy Caprice, who had now been on the road for twenty-six hours straight, simply goes to sleep and changes it all forever. With John asleep, the dead-sticked Caprice crossed the grassy median and, with less than a second's notice, rammed into the Cayce family of three who were safely cocooned in their seat belts.

John's life ended as he sailed through the windshield. He hated seat belts.

Strapped into the backseat, Ginger was miraculously unscathed; Lauren would escape with only lacerations and severe damage that included a probable permanent loss of hearing in her left ear;

Jerry was not only bashed, cut, and bruised, the blow of his head hitting the side window when the Chevy slammed into his door would put him in a coma for the next week. When he'd finally regained consciousness, he was moved to a private sanatorium at the doctor's suggestion. He needed to be watched carefully for a week, or so, to make sure he didn't relapse.

Lauren had been by his side shortly after he'd awakened. A week later, after he'd been moved to the private hospital, she'd left for New York City for an operation on her ear. Columbia University was pioneering a new surgery that might restore her hearing. She was going to postpone it, but Jerry had talked her into going. The surgeon was usually scheduled weeks ahead of time and a slot had opened up for her.

Larry was taking time off to go with her. She would be there for a week, staying in the hospital hospice, checking in for a few minutes daily so the surgeons could monitor the progress. Larry was going to stay with an old college buddy. There were some longtime musician friends who had left Nashville for the Big Apple. Lauren promised Jerry she would look them up.

Some close friends were taking care of Ginger, and except for a few visitors, Jerry was left alone to rest. The boxes marked "POLICE" ceased to turn up, and no more musicians were reported missing.

CHAPTER NINETEEN

I

A friend brought Jerry home from the private hospital about eight-thirty in the morning. They had kept him under observation for three weeks instead of the expected one week. Lauren had called his room very early to say she was with a dying patient at Centennial.

After front-door assurances, Jerry was left alone. By ten o'clock, he'd decided that getting out of the house would be best. He got in the car, drove around for a while, then went to three back-to-back movies.

Depression had flickered at the fringes all day. He told himself over and over that he was not responsible for what was going on. But the depression he battled during the day was nothing compared to the overwhelming onslaught Lauren would deliver when he arrived home at six o'clock.

"Jerry, where the hell have you been?"

"I went to the movies." He was noticeably taken back.

She screamed at him. "The whole goddamn world is going to Hell on the handlebars, and you go to the fucking movies!" It was out of character for Lauren. Freckles were obliterated by red rage.

"I read the paper. I was depressed. I got out of the house."

"Let's go in the den. I want you to sit down. I've got to talk to you." She calmed a little.

The only sound on the way into the den was the swishing of her hose.

"Sit." He did. She stood with her arms folded across her chest and continued. "The cops have been here four times today. They wouldn't let me leave the house."

"Why? What do they want?"

"They're after you. They're going to arrest you for all this killing. They said if you came home, that you'd better turn yourself in. It'd be much easier on you."

"Why do they want me, Lauren?"

"I suspect it's because while you were in the hospital, the killings stopped." Jerry had been forwarding his rough drafts to John Fawley's department as he wrote them.

"That's ridiculous. You can alibi me for most of those other murders. I have one or two other alibis." His facial expression now looked like it was beginning to show critical damage. The dark eyes darted, his oversized lips pursed constantly.

"Not anymore, Jerry. They grilled the hell out of

me. I had to tell them that in a lot of those instances, I was lying."

"Lying! Jesus, Lauren. Why did you tell them that?"

"Because I was. I don't know where you were most of those times."

"Oh, my God . . ."

"They don't believe your other alibis either."

"Jesus Christ, Lauren. That's murder one—the electric chair! You hung me out to dry!" He sounded like he was on the verge of tears. He leaped from the chair and began to pace. His sanity appeared to be swishing around like a toilet flushing. She did nothing to comfort him.

"Jerry, I'm filing for divorce."

He turned and screamed, "Lauren!"

This must be what it looks like to see a person's shell cracking into tiny rivulets. All that's lacking is the crackling sound.

She went on.

"Jerry, you know I've never been in love with you. I told you years ago that I wanted a man who would be faithful. You have been, and I appreciate that. But since we've been apart this last month, I've had a lot of time to think."

"Think about what, Lauren? You're my wife— the mother of our child!"

"There's someone else, and I'm deeply in love with him."

"I can't believe this. In five minutes, the whole fucking world has just blown apart."

"I'll sleep in the spare room tonight. Tomorrow, I've made arrangements to move to an apartment. Ginger will go with me."

He dived to his knees in front of her and grabbed her white uniform in both hands.

"Lauren, you can't do this! This is a nightmare." He screamed, and she backed away, pulling his hands from her dress. "How can you dump all this on me at once? You know what it can do to me!"

"You're a big boy. You'll figure the way out of it."

Still on his knees, he doubled over in obvious pain. He sobbed, "Lauren, please don't do this!" With a more sobered voice, he cried, "Please don't go through with it."

Lauren was in the doorway. She turned and said, "I've got to go back to the hospital and get my briefcase. I'll be back in an hour."

She walked out of the room leaving him in what appeared to be an utter state of destruction.

II

One hour later Lauren arrived home. Even though it had got dark, the lights in the house had not been turned on. She wondered if he had done it.

As she walked in the side door, she heard the shot.

She rushed up the stairs to the attic and found him twitching on the floor. Blood poured from the side of his head where a huge hole appeared. There was a large splatter of blood on the wall and a potted rubber tree that stood in the corner next to the dormer. There was no note.

Lauren calmly picked up the phone and dialed a number.

"He did it. The little wimp finally did it." There was a short silence as the person on the other end said something, then she said, "I'll go get him. Just be ready."

It was just after eight o'clock when Lauren walked into the side entrance of the private hospital. There was no one in the hall. If someone did stop her, she was there to see Mrs. Braddish, an elderly woman whom she had been counseling for the past six months. It was the same hospital Jerry had just left that morning. Most of the beds were taken up with patients with permanent brain damage or passive mental problems.

She'd first met *him* the day she'd been talking to Mrs. Braddish in the physical therapy room. One of the therapists was exercising the elderly lady's arthritic fingers after coating them with an ointment. They'd brought him into the room in a wheelchair and helped him onto the table. Empty eyes stared at the ceiling as the therapist cycled his limbs through patterns designed to keep the unused muscles toned.

Lauren had remained after they'd taken Mrs. Braddish to her room. She'd seen other catatonics, but for some reason she was drawn to this giant of a man.

His hair was coal-shine black. A thin, hawked nose separated glassy, emerald-green eyes that rarely blinked. Steam shovel hands lay cupped on a thick forest of black hair on his chest. He was wearing blue sweat pants with a green stripe up the side. His shirt had been removed for the exercises and massage that was to come. His torso was enormous. The man must have been six-feet-six, or seven.

His therapist turned to Lauren and said, "Mrs. Cayce, could you keep an eye on him for a minute? I've got to go get the heat vibrator, and it's at the other end of the building."

"Jonna, what is his case history? Why's he here?"

"Oh, he's been here for almost twenty years. He was a brilliant musician. Supposedly, he killed his mother, but before they could hang it on him, he went catatonic. They think he was a sociopath— that he had been killing people since he was a kid. He's never caused us any trouble or tried to escape."

"Is he cyclic?"

"Yes. He has some good days. He can walk, and he'll talk a little once in a while. Some of the doctors think he's been faking it for years, but they can't prove it. If they thought he was better, they'd arrest him and try him for murder. If he's faking, he's real good at it."

"What's his name?"

"Ron Creed."

Ron Creed! My God, does Jerry . . .

Lauren entered his room. He was sitting in a chair in the dark, waiting for her. She'd told him that morning that it'd probably be tonight. The bed was already stuffed with pillows and towels to make it look like he was sleeping with the blanket over his head. It was not the first time he'd sneaked out over the years. Because he'd been careful, he'd never been caught.

They went out the side door, got in her car, unseen, and drove off.

A block down the street, Lauren turned and said vehemently, "Darling, he was still using your name. He said it helped him focus better—that he would have the computer go through the manuscript and change it to something else when he was finished. Can you imagine the nerve of the little . . . He was still using your real name."

The big man lifted a huge hand and caressed her hair.

"It's all right. He's dead. We'll write the note.

Six months from now, we'll be in the Carribean on our honeymoon."

She turned to him and smiled. "Darling, I can't wait. I love you so much. I still can't believe the incredible coincidence. I knew Jerry was originally from Texas, and I knew he had been in several bands in high school. But he never once mentioned that the *real* Ron Creed was in them, too. And your mom . . ."

"The slut. You can believe me. She as much as admitted it, too." Creed's teeth became clenched and his speech tightened. "The bitch! She was twenty years older than Jerry was. How could she do something like that—with a kid—with one of my best friends? I saw him leaving across the back lawn one time in the dark. I know it was him. I had all I could do while he was in the sanatorium to keep from cutting the little creep to shreds."

"It's okay, darling. Calm down. It was a long time ago. You gave her exactly what she deserved."

"That's sure as shit."

"This way you're going to get out. You'll finally be free."

When they reached the attic room, Jerry was still laying in a puddle of blood. Lauren turned on the computer and booted it up. Creed stood staring at the body with hate. It was lying mostly hidden in the shadow of the large pot and its rubber tree.

Lauren turned to the big man and said, "Okay, Ron, darling, I've got to have the details of how you killed her to make them believe this—something that wasn't in the paper."

"That's easy, Lauren. The one thing I did that never was put in any of the papers was cut out her asshole. The bitch."

Jerry's suicide confession slowly began to take shape on the screen.

Dear Lauren,

Please forgive me, but I can't live with the guilt of all these killings anymore, and I can't stop myself. Something else has been bothering me a long time. My first murder was when I was in high school. I killed the mother of one of my best friends. We were having an affair, and she said she was breaking it off. There was a knife, and I just went berserk. I couldn't stop myself then either. I even cut out her rectum. The friend's name was Ron Creed. The last I knew, he was still in a hospital. The police were always sure he had done it, but with this truth, maybe it will help him recover and live a normal life.

Good-bye Lauren. I love you and Ginger, but this way is best.

Creed read it, turned to her, and said, "That's

perfect, Lauren. In the next month, the police are going to see one helluva miraculous recovery."

He put his arms around her and said, "I want to make love to you, Lauren."

"Not now, darling. We've got to get you out of here, and I've got to call the police."

"No. I want to do it now . . . like we did when I first met you. The police can wait."

"Ron, somebody could come in. One of the neighbors could drop by. We'll have plenty of time later."

"No, Lauren. It's got to be now."

He grabbed her by the arm and roughly pulled her toward the stairs.

In a few minutes, flesh could be heard slapping in dull thumps. Creed's pumping grew more and more violent. Lauren began to cry in pants as the big man's grunts became louder and louder. He slammed into her with fury, faster, faster. His weight and the vigor of his thrust pushed her head against the bed's headboard. Bracing her hands against the wood to ease the battering, she finally cried, "I'm coming, Ron! You're so wonderful! I'm going to come! Oh, God. I'm going to come."

"Hi, Ron. Long time no see." The voice came from the foot of the bed.

Lauren screamed, bucked, and pushed the big man off. Creed rolled onto his back beside her, his tumescence ejaculating into the air in great white spurts.

"Oh, dear. You've made another mess, Ronnie."

"You're so wonderful? Jesus, Lauren. You never said that to me." Jerry stood there with a grin on his face. He was holding a 9mm automatic. There was another gun in his belt, a revolver.

"Oh, my God, you're dead!" Lauren made no attempt to cover her nakedness. She was shocked and visibly shaken.

Jerry walked to the side of the bed, just out of Creed's reach. His face was plastered in blood, and there was still a large hole in the side of his head.

He took a hand towel from Lauren's dressing table and began wiping the blood from his face.

"Chicken blood. Got it at a slaughterhouse. I was afraid you'd smell catsup or the stuff from the theater supply."

Lauren was open-mouthed speechless. Creed's reaction was anger—gradually—seething.

"Oh, sorry. I must look a mess." Jerry reached to his head and pulled the hole off in one motion. It now became an obvious rubber mask that slipped over one side of his head. He continued wiping off the blood.

"Well, Ronnie, I haven't seen you in a lot of years. I guess the last time was when you almost walked in on me and your dear momma fucking our brains out. I just barely got away." The gun never wavered.

"You son of a bitch!"

Lauren said nothing.

"Hey Ron, no big deal. She was a whore. She was fucking half the guys in town." He began laughing at the big man. Creed's anger was quickly coming to a boil.

"Listen, I hope you don't mind my using your name and a few of your escapades in my new book. I changed it a little—to say you didn't care much about your mother—rather than being in love with her. Talk about Oedipus Rex! Of course, you get the booby prize in the end. Speaking of boobies, I'll say this, Creed: your mom did have nice boobies. She loved to have two of us suck them simultaneously."

Creed came off the bed with a roar, and the musician backed away and began firing. Some of the shots hit the giant, and charcoaled holes smoked and oozed minimal blood from the cauterized wounds. The big man did not stop or even slow down. Jerry fired the last two shots point blank at Creek's face. The big man was still unfazed as flesh blew off in a cloud of bloody vapor. He reached out and took the redhead by the throat with both hands. With all his strength, Jerry swung the gun and clobbered Creed on the jaw. The giant's eyes rolled, he slowly slumped to the floor and stopped breathing.

The bedroom air was full of cordite. Fortunately, the house was far enough from the road and the neighbors so that the shooting-gallery sounds would go undetected.

Lauren was still sitting in the middle of the bed in shock, her hand clamped to her mouth. Her eyes shouted fear, but she controlled it.

Jerry leaned against the dresser massaging his throat. She didn't move. Finally, he croaked, "Well, darling, here we are alone at last in our own bedroom."

She had composed herself. Her voice was low, furry, laced with sin as she said calmly, "How did you know, Jerry?"

Still massaging his throat and coughing, he tried to get the words out. "Pre- premoni-tion." He gulped and continued, his voice cracking then evening out. "Can you beat that? I just didn't believe it until recently. I caught a few glimpses of what you were up to, and it started to make sen-se."

Still coughing, he took a handkerchief from his back pocket and began wiping off the gun while he continued.

"It wasn't until I saw our friend Ron in the sanatorium a couple weeks ago that I figured out *who* it was. I knew you had a client there. One of the patients told me you and he were very chummy. Why so bitter, Lauren? I've loved you. I've taken care of you well."

She crossed her legs and sat Indian style on the sheet. Looking him in the eye, she spat, "You don't know what love is, Jerry. You don't know what it's like to have to go for years and be denied your worst craving—to be kept from a kind of love this world has rarely seen."

"Bullshit. This moron could never keep you happy. I can't believe the coincidence of you finding the guy I got the idea for my book from. Then you go and fall in love with the bastard. Good God, Lauren, he's a fucking psychopath."

"So am I, Jerry. So is Larry. We killed our slut mother the same way Ron killed his. Maybe that's what fascinated me. We were luckier than he was—the cops wrote our mother off to a burglar."

"I don't believe that, Lauren. I don't believe anything you say now. I sure as hell can't believe you've done this to Ginger and me. You've had me believing you cared, if only a little—for years."

"I'm a good actress, Jerry. Most women are when it comes to fooling men. You were kind, you were wealthy, and you provided me with the security I needed. I finally just got tired of it, and the opportunity presented itself. After you're gone, we'll have your money and the entire pie."

"After I'm gone? Have my money? Got your tenses a little mixed up haven't you?"

Lauren said nothing. She had made no move to get off the bed. Jerry took the other gun from his belt.

"Two guns, Lauren. You're wondering why I didn't use the second one on him. You see, this one will have his finger prints on it. You're going to make me do the hardest thing I've ever done in my life. If it weren't for Ginger . . ." His voice faltered then continued. "I imagine you already knew that this piece of shit on the floor here is the original asshole killer—he's where I got the idea. The cops are going to think he broke in here looking for another arranger to kill, but decided to do a number on you while he was waiting. I came home, unfortunately just after he'd pulled the trigger on you, and sent him to his reward. For all I know, he is the serial killer."

"It won't work, Jerry. You don't have what it takes to do it."

"You're wrong, darling. When I was ten years old, my pony broke his leg in a chuckhole when I was out riding him one day. My father told me it was my horse, I had to be the one to put him down. I can still remember what he said like it was yesterday—'Son, sometimes there are things that just have to be done no matter how badly we don't want to do them—things that leave you no choice.' I did it, Lauren. I never would have thought that I was capable, but when your back's up against the wall, you can do a lot of things. There's no way you can live, and me not go to the electric chair now. I just killed this maniac in cold blood as far as the law's concerned. When it's a matter of life and death for Ginger and me, by God, we're gonna live!" His face scrunched in concentrated contempt. "There's no way I could ever trust you now. I've tried to believe I could for years, but this bullshit—you went too far and now it's a matter of self-defense. Self-preservation is the strongest instinct possessed by any living organism, Lauren. Besides, think of the sympathy I'll get. It will be tremendously helpful when my book goes on the market." He made imaginary quotation marks in the air as he said, 'Author's wife murdered by killer he invented.' I may be washed up in the music business, Lauren, but I'm going to make it as a writer, and there's nothing that's going to stop me—not even you!"

He raised the gun and cocked the hammer. Fear came into his wife's eyes like the curtains being opened on a movie screen. It dawned on her that he really was going through with it. She screamed as he leveled the gun and squeezed the trigger.

A shot exploded from the doorway first, and Jerry fell over backward. His head smacked the dresser's edge with a loud splat as he slumped to the floor.

"Goddamn you, Larry! Where have you been!"

"Well, baby, I saw him come down the stairs, but I couldn't very well shoot him while you were entertaining his friend here, could I? Mr. Creed would have wondered how your loving husband had managed to die twice."

"Jesus. The bastard almost did it! If you'd been half a second slower."

"I knew what I was doing. I would never let anything happen to you, sweetheart."

"Did you see what he pulled? I never would have thought he had the guts!"

"Ain't life a juicy surprise? In spite of Jerry screwing up as usual, we've still done it. Your husband, the arranger, is killed by the serial murderer, whom you manage to shoot with great difficulty. Now, we have the money, enough so that we can do anything we please. And . . . starting right now . . ." He laid the gun down and walked toward her unbuttoning his jeans. ". . . I am going to personally fuck my twin sister's brains out every night of the week. Nobody could fault family for moving in after what you've been through." She smiled in eager expectation.

It was absurdly incongruous in a room filled with death, but, naked and relieved, she smiled and opened her arms and legs to the love of her life—the only love she'd ever known, a love begun as near-identical embryos in her mother's twice-cursed uterus. "God, I want you! Bring a wet cloth and wash that ape off me first."

CHAPTER TWENTY

I

It was different with the twins—kisses, caresses, tenderness. This was a love that had been consummated over and over since they were ten years old. It built slowly. There would be no faking orgasm this time. For this, she had pushed Jerry to suicide and lured Creed to his sacrificial death. The mental patient would be revealed as the serial killer who had climaxed the city's horror with the murder of the author himself. She must remember to plant the house and burglar alarm key in Creed's pants. She had already notified the sanatorium that she thought she had lost them there.

Larry had just entered her when Lauren felt the mattress dip in a place it shouldn't have. She opened her eyes in time to see a huge, bloody hand grip the side of the bed. It was followed by half of a blubbering, bloody face.

She screamed as the weeping turned to a hoarse growl, and the giant stood up. Larry was just a hair too slow reacting, and Creed grabbed

259

the twin's neck like a dead game bird and gave it a sharp twist. There was an accompanying grinding sound and Larry went limp, eyes bulging in fear. Creed threw him onto the floor as Lauren grabbed Larry's gun from the bedside table. There were thirteen shots left in the 9mm, and she kept firing until the gun was empty. The giant collapsed across her legs on the bed, splattering blood and erupted tissue. This time he was dead.

Lauren laid the gun down and wriggled from beneath him. She slid off the bed to the floor next to Larry. She was numbed. It had happened too fast. There was no pulse in her twin.

The realization slowly built, blowing through her mind like a morning breeze replacing stale night air. She began to moan softly, swaying, holding his head in her lap. There were no tears.

"No. No. No, no, no, baby."

Jerry's second gun had dropped to the floor near where she sat. It took little effort to reach it. She kissed her brother a last time, placed the muzzle under her chin and fired without a second's hesitation.

II

"Mr. Cayce, I don't know what happened before you killed that maniac. Evidently he found your wife and her brother here instead of you and tried to make them do some kind of sex act while he waited. Evidently Larry refused to go through with it, so Creed broke his neck, raped Lauren, and then shot her. You said you emptied two clips into him?"

"Yeah. Lucky I grabbed the extra one when I took the gun from the downstairs closet. He just kept coming."

"We still haven't found all the holes."

Jerry was sure they wouldn't run ballistic tests on the slugs. All the bullets in Creed were 9mm, but they came from two different guns.

Jerry looked at the suspicious cop through bloodshot eyes. The two men were in the kitchen, Jerry seated at the breakfast table with a fresh cup of coffee in front of him. It had been a long night. The bottom line was that everything fit well enough for the police not to be able to prove otherwise.

The author compared this man to the cop in his book. There really wasn't much similarity. This guy was a Yale graduate, a criminology Ph.D. in a three-piece suit. The names had only been another of Sam's remarkable coincidences.

"Well, it looks like we've finally got our serial killer."

Fawley didn't know it, but Jerry had a terrific headache from hitting his head on the dresser as he had fallen. It had knocked him cold. His side still smarted from the hot groove Larry's bullet had burned. Thank goodness, Larry had always been a lousy shot. Anyway, what Fawley didn't know, wouldn't hurt him.

"Are you going to be okay?"

"Yeah. I took a tranquilizer. What am I going to tell my daughter? That's the hardest part." To himself, he thought, "I sure as hell know what I'm not going to tell you. You'd have me in jail for the attempted murder of my darling wife, in addition to goading that poor fool into charging—that's murder in the first and second degree at least."

"I'm sorry, Mr. Cayce. It always seems to be the hardest on the kids. Will you finish the book?"

"I don't know, Lieutenant. It'll be a while, if I do."

"Are you sure you don't want me to call someone?"

He shook his head sadly. "No. There's no one."

The cop left the room, and Jerry's mind returned to when he'd regained consciousness.

He'd glimpsed Larry's smile just before he'd hit his head on the dresser, so he knew who had shot him. When he'd awakened, Creed was on the bed, Larry was lying naked in Lauren's lap on the floor, his neck twisted at a ridiculous angle, and the top of Lauren's head was all over the ceiling. Jerry had rearranged the bodies to support what he would tell the police.

Head throbbing, he'd taken the rubber mask to the bathroom and cut it into tiny pieces with a razor blade before flushing it down the john. Then he'd gone back up into the attic, cleaned up the catsup and deleted the suicide note on the word processor. He took all the blood-covered towels downstairs, threw them in the washer with detergent and turned it on. Getting his story straight in his mind, he'd finally called the police.

III

The police had all left by noon. The three bodies had been removed in green plastic body bags. The lieutenant said his good-byes, gave Jerry further condolences, and left. Except for Ginger, who was still at the home of friends, Jerry was alone in the world for the first time in twelve years. It hurt, but not the way he knew it would when the shock wore off.

It had taken awhile, but he'd finally figured out the plot. With what had happened in the bedroom, and the things he'd known about Lauren and Larry for years, the scenario developed in his mind as if he were writing it as the last chapter of a book.

* * *

"Well, Mr. Cayce, you won't have to worry about the copycat killer anymore. The lunatic is dead. Who'd have thought an old grudge would have sprung off your wife working in that sanatorium. He must have overheard her talking about you and your book, stolen her keys, then sneaked out and got into your computer for all those months. It's a wonder he wasn't caught breaking into your house."

"Lieutenant, you're wrong. Creed wasn't the killer. Check with his doctors, you'll see."

The cop looked puzzled.

"Would you explain?"

"Lauren's brother, Larry, was the copycat killer. He was trying to drive me to suicide. Lauren knew I've had a life-long problem with depression—I even tried to commit suicide when I was younger."

"Suicide? This is quite a revelation. Continue, Mr. Cayce."

"They thought that all those murders would place a tremendous responsibility on my shoulders. She had been dumping on me periodically to break me down—whenever I'd get depressed, she'd level another howitzer and fire. Yesterday morning, she went for broke when she told me the cops were after me and that she was filing for divorce. If I didn't kill myself, she had poor Creed, a known sociopath, all primed to do the job anyway. I was getting to the end of the book. She had to act or the opportunity would be gone."

* * *

Jerry thought to himself, "If I hadn't committed that faked suicide, that's how it would have read. Ingenious, how she lured the big man to the house. She'd promised that my suicide confession would free the poor sap from the sanatorium and a murder rap. And the promise of herself . . ."

He got up from the table, threw the cold coffee in the sink, and got a refill.

". . . *Then she or Larry would have killed Creed in the act of cutting out the asshole of the author of* The Famous Asshole Murders, *subtitle,* How to Relieve Constipation in One Easy Try. *The police would think the killer was dead—end of case—don't look any further, thank you—Elvis has left the building.*"

"*And she would have been right, Mr. Cayce. Please continue.*"

"*Trying to force me into suicide didn't work because after thinking it through, I really didn't feel responsible. I didn't have all that guilt they thought I did. I was writing a good book. I thought if some maniac wants to act out these murders, it's not my fault. Now that I see who the maniac was, and why he was doing it, I know it was selfish and that I was wrong.*"

To himself the author said, "*Bullshit. It's great publicity and will net me a best-seller.*"

Out loud, he continued, "*Had I quit, it might have saved a lot of lives.*"

Fawley was standing in a corner of the kitchen with a cup of coffee. "That's for certain."

"I didn't completely catch on to what she was pulling until she told me that the cops were going to arrest me for the murders. I knew that wasn't true because I had just left you in your office."

Jerry broke his reverie and got up from the table once again. This time he threw the fresh coffee in the sink and rinsed the cup. He went to the refrigerator and filled the cup with orange juice.

The charade infringed once again, and the narrative continued as if he were writing out this new book—New Book—there had to be a plot in here somewhere for the next novel.

"Would you like some orange juice, Lieutenant?"

"No. Thanks."

"There are other reasons why Larry committed the copycat murders from my manuscript. By the way, what Lauren didn't show him, he got first hand off the word processor disks when nobody was home. He had both the house and burglar alarm keys, and Lauren had found my hiding place for the desk key. Even if she had been feeding Creed the information, she never met Creed until after you had discovered the bodies in the swamp. Yesterday I checked on her counseling records to see when she first went to that sanatorium. Also, Creed was truly catatonic a lot of the time. The doctors have confirmed that."

"This is really eye-opening, Mr. Cayce. What are the other reasons?"

"Okay. First, you have to understand that neither Lauren nor Larry were normal. They were both under the care of a psychiatrist—had been for years. Lauren didn't like to admit it, but she still took medication. The real pisser is that they had been lovers for years."

"My God! Go on."

"She was a beautiful woman, Lieutenant. How do you think a klutz like me could get a woman like that to marry him unless there was something wrong with her?"

"I'm not sure I know what you mean, but go on."

"I met Lauren in college and fell hopelessly in love with her. It was a case of the toad and the princess. Can you imagine how incredible I felt like when she agreed to marry me?"

"I guess."

Jerry continued, "The problem was, there were rumors that she and her brother were a little strange. Most of the guys were afraid of her. I found out after we'd been dating for a while that whenever she went out with a guy, Larry would turn up and kick the shit out of him. She never seemed to mind. I guess she thought that it was a test of their love—she knew Larry loved her if he wouldn't let anybody else have her. However, he let her go out with me. I was the toad. I didn't threaten their relationship. I also came from a very wealthy background. Larry knew *she would be financially secure and always looked after. They could continue their love affair on the side and have the best of both worlds. They were sick."*

"Love affair? With her twin brother? That's very sick!"

"I know." Jerry released a great sigh that mixed remorse and shame.

"How did you find out about all this?"

"I hadn't completely taken leave of my senses. Before we were married, I had a private investigator look into their background. The two of them had been in trouble from the time they were kids. Mostly, it was things like hanging the neighbors' cats or setting fire to dogs."

"That's usually the way it begins."

"Yes. The police in their hometown were almost sure they murdered their mother, but it could never be proven. They alibied each other."

"Weren't you frightened? You were married to her for what . . . ten, twelve years, weren't you?"

"I was never frightened. You have to realize I really loved her. And I thought she cared for me—at least some. It's even possible that Ginger is really my daughter. Lauren wanted a child almost as badly as she wanted her brother, and I don't think she would have had the nerve to allow Larry to be a father— the inbreeding problems . . . Anyway, I knew they would never touch me because it was the only way they could keep their affair going and still remain secure. They wouldn't kill the sugar daddy."

"What about Larry's other reasons for all the killings?" Fawley had put away his notebook.

The author combed his hair with his hand and continued. "In the beginning, I truly believe that Larry was trying to dig up publicity for my book. It would mean a lot more money for Lauren."

"That's a helluva thin reason."

"It's worse than that when you realize that my family left me very well off. The book wouldn't have made that much difference."

"Any more reasons?"

"Yes. He just loved to kill. Here was a ready-made blueprint. All he had to do was find the victim and do it." To himself, Jerry continued, "And I'll go to the electric chair before I ever tell you that my first drafts contained the names of the real musicians I personally would liked to have seen dead in my cathartic little adventure. Those disks were the ones left in the desk—all changed now, including Ron Creed—by means of "search" and "replace" in the word processing program. Too bad it didn't double and triple the number of my sessions like it did Creed's in the book!"

The lieutenant digested the words for a few seconds, then said, "I only have a couple more questions."

"Yes."

"Why go through the elaborate scheme of trying to make you commit suicide? Why didn't Larry shoot you and make it look like suicide?"

"I think Lauren wouldn't let him go that far. There was a limit. I'd like to think that she had to care some. In her twisted mind, she didn't want to live the rest of her life knowing that her brother had killed the father of her daughter."

"Okay, then why didn't she just let Creed do the job?"

"He was unreliable. She undoubtedly would have tried to get him to if I hadn't faked the suicide. Either way, my death would be pinned on him. Suicide would allow Lauren to inherit, but she wouldn't collect any life insurance. When Creed came on the scene, they saw that they might be able to hang my death on him in order to collect the life insurance, too—over three million dollars worth!"

"Ah. I see. Now it's beginning to become clear."

"Creed turned out to be icing on the cake. That's all. I'm sure they played with him like a cat batting around a dying mouse. Through the years, Lieutenant, Lauren did some nasty things—not physical things—Larry was the one into the physical side of hurting. She was into mental pain. I think the most important reason she was a counselor for the dying was because she enjoyed watching the people suffer."

Jerry was tired of the scenario. He was tired of life. The permanence of tragedy was beginning to set up like four-hour cement. Maybe he could lose himself in the book.

He started for the attic. He would just write a

little while, then go get Ginger. He hadn't figured out yet what to tell her.

Climbing the stairs with his life on the edge of tears, he heard himself say softly, "God, Laura, I miss you already."

CHAPTER TWENTY-ONE

I

The sanatorium's thick carpet swallowed his footfalls as Dr. Thomas Arquette climbed the steps of the elaborate foyer. Overhead a gigantic chandelier reflected the brass light effused by three-story bronzed windows. Had he turned around, the view would have been breathtaking. Expensive horse farms with fields carefully gift wrapped in snow and tied with ribbons of white fences shared the vista with patches of woods, interesting hills, and a lake.

Before him, ornate banisters outlined the two diverging stairways that curved upward from the foyer to the mezzanine. The walls were elaborately paneled in sections framed with decorative moldings. Original oils marched up the stairs alongside the young psychiatrist by the light of their own brass lamps.

The facility was not large—only two floors that housed less than thirty patients. The administration had kept it small to cater to a few wealthy clients rather than many who were not. Care was the finest money could buy. Nothing was spared. The patients' suites resembled those of an expensive penthouse.

The doctor reached the mezzanine and was confronted by a reception area dwarfed by more chandeliers. The receptionist belonged on the cover of *Vogue*. She was stunning, her coiffeured-brunet hair set off by a royal-blue designer dress and thick gold necklaces and bracelets.

The thirty-three-year-old man, who had spent most of his life in sterile schools and institutions, was not immune to such splendor. He croaked, "I'm Doctor Arquette. I'm supposed to meet Dr. Bruckstein."

"How do you do, Doctor Arquette. I'm Emily Dickinson." She stood and the dazzling smile was accompanied by the reassuring offer of her hand.

"The real Emily Dickinson?" he quipped as he tentatively took the hand.

"Close—a great-granddaughter." Even the smile was expensive. "We've been expecting you. Dr. Bruckstein's office is the third door on the right. I'll buzz them." She pointed down the hall. The psychiatrist had difficulty turning away, and as if sensing it, she said, "I'll see you later this afternoon at the cocktail party—in your honor."

The smile lingered on his mind for fifty feet after he had mumbled a thank-you and had started down the hall.

"We really are glad to have you here," she called. "I've heard about your work."

He turned back awkwardly and answered, "Thank you. I'll look forward to talking with you later."

He walked through an ornate arch into a large outer office and was confronted by another receptionist, this one twenty years older than the first but still as attractive.

"Good morning, Dr. Arquette. Dr. Bruckstein?" She had been waiting for him.

A small, distinguished-looking gentleman with a file in his hand was speaking to a secretary at her desk in one corner of the room. What little hair he had was neatly trimmed and of the purest white. Rimless glasses and a navy pinstriped suit gave him the unmistaking appearance of the modicum of propriety. He looked up, then quickly moved across the room to meet the new doctor. Hand outstretched, his smile set several crow's-feet in bas-relief. He piped with obvious pleasure, "I'm Samuel Bruckstein, Doctor Arquette. We are so happy to have a man of your stature joining us. Please come into my office. Let's chat."

"Thank you, sir."

As he closed the door to his office, he said, "Ordinarily, I would have interviewed you myself, but Gordon recommended you so highly, and your publications and reputation . . ."

II

At the end of the third day, the two psychiatrists had come to the last patient in the hospital. Dr. Bruckstein entered the spacious suite while opening the case file in his hand. The immediate room was split into two levels and was sumptuously decorated with hand-stenciled wallpapers and ornate moldings. The windows were elegantly dressed, and the furniture would only be found in the most expensive mansions.

A small, pale man about five-feet-six, and who could have weighed no more than one hundred twenty-five pounds was sitting on a thirty-thousand-dollar *Saporiti Italia* leather sofa on the lower level. Brown hair was medium length and nicely styled; facial features were regular with nothing to designate him as handsome or homely. He was dressed in tan slacks and a red cashmere pullover. *Air Nikes* were flat on the floor, his arms were in his lap, and his stare was at a wall covered with tiny foxhunt scenes. A television set was playing *Music City Tonight,* picture only. On one side of the room there was an elaborate stereo component system. A Beethoven piano sonata played softly. The man did not react to the two doctors entering the million-dollar suite.

A nurse was attempting to feed him. She was strikingly beautiful—blond, hazel-eyed, freckled.

Sitting down, her short nurse's dress was pulled most of the way up her thighs. It was evident that she was perfectly proportioned and filled the uniform in all the regulation places.

The men heard her say, "If you refuse to eat your peas, I won't let you watch the football game. Open up big." She spooned in a load of peas.

"Hello, Doctors." As if apologizing, she made a face and said, "He hates peas, but it's good for him to not get his own way all the time."

"Hello, Laura. Can't talk him into a night on the town, huh?"

"Don't I wish." There was a giggle, and her face broke into a stunning smile.

"Shame on a woman who just got married."

She grinned sinfully, and said, "I tried to hold out for him, but he just wouldn't ask me."

The doctor laughed genuinely, the nurse smiled. He introduced the new doctor to her, they shook hands, then she returned her attention to feeding the man sitting in the chair one last spoonful of peas.

The two men watched as she busied herself with cleaning up. Finally straightening, she sighed and said to the new doctor, "He's a pistol, Doctor Arquette. A real pistol. I'm looking forward to working with you. Maybe you can help him."

"We'll certainly try, Laura."

She collected the tray, looked back at the sitting man once more, smiled, and left the room.

The older doctor turned to face the patient and said, "Dr. Arquette, this last gentleman on our tour is a classic catatonic schizophrenic. He'd already been here two years when I arrived. He'll turn thirty-eight next month.

"He lost his father when he was three years old—heart attack. He was raised by his mother and grandfather, and we understand he was an extraordinarily talented musician—a child prodigy. His IQ had been measured at over one hundred ninety, and we know from records that he had a photographic memory.

"They were absolutely certain that he murdered his mother. Only one week before her murder, his grandfather, who was old Texas oil, had committed suicide—shot himself in the head, and, I might add, under a cloud of suspicion. With the grandfather gone, his mother was a very wealthy woman—for one week! With *her* dead, he was, and still is, the sole survivor of the estate, which is worth well over two hundred million dollars. Unless he's convicted, the state can't take his money. Because he hasn't moved a muscle on his own in twenty years, they can't even prosecute."

Dr. Arquette interrupted, "Murdered his mother?"

Dr. Bruckstein continued, "According to the records of his psychiatrist, he'd been under suspicion for a number of murders all the way back to age six. They thought he might have pushed a three-year-old into a swimming pool.

"I flew to Texas several years ago to talk with the family doctor. He told me they could never find proof. If he was killing people, he was much too clever to get caught."

"My God. Six years old. That may be a new one for the books—sociopath at six. It usually takes years to develop that kind of personality."

"Yes. And he evidently had an elaborate scheme worked out to get away with his mother's murder."

"How's that?"

"He was playing for a dance about ten miles from his home. The band usually took a fifteen to twenty-minute break every hour or so. He'd secretly bought one of those high-powered sport motorcycles—one that even back then would do well over a hundred miles an hour?"

"I've seen them. Dangerous. And . . ."

"They speculated that he had it hidden somewhere near the dance and was going to sprint home in the early morning hours, kill his mother, then sprint back to the dance and later get rid of the motorcycle. Iffy, but possible. The police would have determined it impossible for him to travel ten miles, commit the murder, then travel ten miles back to the dance and do it in twenty minutes."

"Why didn't he get away with it?"

"They found him sitting on the front steps, the bike parked in the shrubbery. He was exactly like you see him now—fully catatonic—that in itself is a miracle."

"Yes, in that short amount of time."

"Evidently, something snapped. He made a bloodbath out of the entire house. There were parts of her body lying in almost every room. He had even cut out her anus."

"My God. How old was he?"

"He'd turned eighteen the week before."

The older doctor then asked the patient, "Ron, would you like to go out on the balcony for a while?" The older doctor found a coat in one of the closets. As he was putting it on the sitting man, he said, "We usually let him sit on the balcony awhile after the noon meal." He slowly and carefully got the man to his feet, then seated him in a wheelchair. Dr. Arquette followed them onto the deck overlooking the beautiful snowy farmland. The temperature was in the fifties—not uncomfortable.

The younger doctor walked over to the sitting man, took an arm, and slowly raised it to a vertical position. It remained extended, perfectly frozen, as he withdrew the support.

Dr. Bruckstein verified, "Complete rigor."

"Yes." The younger doctor replaced the arm in the man's lap and asked, "He's been catatonic for twenty years?"

Dr. Bruckstein answered, "Yes. Other than to

eat, he never moves a muscle by himself. We sit him on the john, bathe, shave him."

"No periodic consciousness cycles?"

"No—again atypical. We've tried every treatment known to man—drugs, electroshock, forced physical exercise accompanied by artificial stress, programmed conditioning by way of television monitors and multimedia slides—bombarding his visual and auditory senses. We've even attempted several experimental drugs. He's never responded to anything in all this time. So, what we've ended up doing is making him as comfortable as possible—I suppose in case any of the outside world filters in."

"How do you mean?"

"Well, I don't know of any other private hospitals where a catatonic schizophrenic would get the treatment he gets. The nurses turn on the Monday Night Football games; they play the stereo—everything from Barbra Streisand to Barbara Mandrell, Brahms, Chopin—books on cassette. Sometimes, they bring him a new movie for the VCR. He spends a lot of time on the balcony during the summer. It's wonderfully peaceful around here—there's the lake, lots of whispering pine trees, squirrels, birds. In fact, there are a couple of mockingbird nests just a few yards from here." He pointed to a bare tree and said, "There's one in that old oak tree. You can just make it out."

The younger man followed the finger as the older doctor continued.

"The guy's estate is paying an arm and a leg. We do all we can to earn it. Who knows, maybe he's taking it all in."

"What about his EEGs? Is there brain activity? Is he thinking?"

"Oh, yes! You better believe it! There've been times when the spikes go right off the paper. Sometimes they resemble the pattern of tremendous creativity—a painter, composer. He's no vegetable. He could be playing his music inside there—writing a symphony. With *his* mind, God only knows."

The older doctor bent to the man sitting in the chair and said, "Mr. Creed, how are you doing in there?" He squatted in front of the frozen man to intercept the unfocused stare as he had done hundreds of times over the years. "Why won't you ever talk to us? We know you're thinking in there. Do you realize how long it's been?"

Dr. Arquette had been leafing through the file. He looked up after studying one of the EEG tapes and said, "You certainly have to wonder what all that brain activity reflects."

"I've wondered a thousand times."

The younger doctor went on, "There is a new drug that's been tried in advanced cases like this in Europe. It's a fourth-generation derivative of Thorazine. They're not sure how it works, but there's been a considerable degree of success with it. It might be . . ."

"Dr. Bruckstein?" A nurse had appeared in the doorway. "Pardon me for interrupting, but there is an important phone call in your office."

"Thank you, Ginger." He turned to the new doctor and said, "It's Larry Khourey. He's the chairman of the board. He calls every Tuesday at this time. Please excuse me. I'll be back in a few minutes."

"Certainly." The soon-to-retire psychiatrist left to talk to his boss.

Dr. Arquette continued to study the past procedures in Ronald David Creed's file. When he looked up to study the man himself, Creed was glaring at him, clear-eyed, unwavering.

"Leave me alone, you asshole!" he hissed. "My world is a thousand times better than your pathetic shit-covered existence."

The hair on the back of the doctor's neck stood on end and danced. The venom and intention in the voice was blood-curdling. It surprised and frightened the psychiatrist so badly, he dropped the file and bolted from the balcony into the room shouting, "Dr. Bruckstein! Dr. Bruckstein!"

He'd flown down the hall and had almost reached the office when the elderly doctor came out the door on a dead run.

"He's talking! He just spoke to me! He's out of the catatonia!"

They ran back to Creed's room and the deck to find him as he had been originally. Frozen, plastic, catatonic. Unshakable.

"But he just turned and spoke to me after you'd left. He told me . . ."

"He told you to leave him alone—his world is better."

"Yes! That's exactly what he said! How did you know?"

"It's what he told me seventeen years ago when I first came here. He hasn't spoken a word since."

"Good Lord!"

"He may be right, Dr. Arquette. Think about it. In his world, he does anything he pleases. Anything! Get the girl every time, murder, rape—play Superman, conduct the London Philharmonic. In our world, he's a sociopath who would quickly be executed for murder or, at best, spend his life in prison or an institution for the criminally insane. Here, we take care of all his physical needs and do it extremely well."

"My God!"

"Haven't you ever awakened in the morning desperately wishing you could return to your dream? I believe our friend here can do it with ease. I'm sure he's refined the reality of his fantasy world far beyond what we can imagine. If I were he—if I had his psychosis, his brain, brilliance; if I could command these circumstances"—he made a sweeping gesture around the room—"and the

284

care . . ." He sighed, and finally said, "I think I'd do exactly what he's done all these years. Wouldn't you?"

III

"Mr. Creed, would you mind if I moved you so I can clean this place up?" The maid had entered with her cleaning cart and a vacuum hose. She slowly stood him up and walked him across the room.

Creed knew she was there, but only barely. He was deep in the coma of his own world. After the shrinks had left, he'd quickly returned to his latest invention—author, extraordinaire, Jerry Cayce! The sniveling little shit was chronicling some of Creed's favorite exploits. In this variation Ronald David Creed played the part of a musician who was killing off his competition—cutting out their assholes in an ultimate sign of contempt for their pathetically inferior abilities. The cops had been chasing him but, as usual, were impotent to catch him whenever he went into survival mode. He wasn't sure about the twist he'd just worked out in Jerry's real life where the twins had used the poor slob from the nuthouse to take the fall. Casting himself as the slobbering giant and letting Jerry, then Lauren, shoot him was certainly different.

"Next run-through, maybe I'll change that. Just make him a nobody." It was a funny feeling— putting himself down for a change.

He had aroused himself to tell the new dip-shit doctor to leave him alone. The stupid bastard needed to be put in his place right at the outset. Let him know who's boss.

"Mr. Creed, I hope you don't mind if I change the channel to the soaps."

The maid went ahead and changed the channel on the television set the same way she did every cleaning day.

"Goddamn twat!"

But returning to the real world for good would be about as sensible as a do-it-yourself lobotomy. Jesus, they'd have him in a cell in a nuthouse or the electric chair before he could say Rambo Reamer. This world had *always* been better than the real one—ever since he had discovered it as a five-year-old kid. Even then they'd tried to take it away from him—making him go to all those god-damn shrinks. In this world, he was in complete control—and he never got caught!

IV

With dolor seeping into his body as slow and sure as August fog, the little author sat for several minutes with his head in his hands. Finally, chubby fingers reached for the keys and the words began their jittery march . . .

Creed was depressed. All the killing should have put him on an incredible high, but instead, a deep and overwhelming foreboding seemed to pervade every pore of his body. Darkness thick enough to cut with a knife had slipped over him like a blanket drenched in melancholy.

He had easily avoided the police. They bored him. Perhaps it was time to go back to work—another city—anywhere he could make music. The urge to play and sing was, at times, overpowering. He missed his grand piano tremendously.

Maybe north. Fresh pastures.

Maybe New York.

I wonder where Laura is right now?